# A Scandalous S
# By Lily Harlem

Other Historical Romance Books By Lily Harlem
Riding With Warriors Trilogy
Head of Household
The Duke's Pet
Shared by the Vikings
Obeying Her Vikings
Claimed by the Clan Chief
Owned by the Highlanders
Mastered by the Viking King
Submitting to the Viking Warrior
The Viking's Captive
Steinn

# Chapter One

Lady Elizabeth Burghley wiped the back of her hand over her brow and paused to listen to the song of a mistle thrush. The day was heating up, even in the shade of the ancient forest that lay just south of Burghley House, but that hadn't stopped the birds from making their music.

And it hadn't deterred her from taking a walk with paper and paints in tow. She'd spent the morning having tea with her mother's friends and listening to them lament her lack of suitors. She didn't know why they cared. It wasn't their ring fingers that were bereft of jewels. It wasn't their diaries that lacked a Big Day.

She paused and carefully manipulated a determined bramble stalk out of her way—its mean spikes just waiting to snag her gown and stockings. The path wasn't well trodden out here, though it was discernable. At the same time last year she'd found wood anemone growing, a carpet of little white faces and a delight to capture in detail. Today she hoped to find more, but as yet, no luck—only garlic, honeysuckle, bellflowers, and woodruff. The woodruff was pretty, a froth of tiny petals that reminded her of a growing white cloud on a blue-skied day. If she was unlucky finding anemone she'd paint woodruff instead.

A scrabble in the undergrowth to her right caught her attention. She paused, staring at the tangle of greenery. What was it? In her mind it was a snake or a rat or perhaps an orange-furred stoat. She held her breath, clutched her painting set in her gloved hands, and stared.

A sudden squawk—the alarm call of a female blackbird—and the creature lifted from the undergrowth with a frantic flap.

"In the name of the good Lord," she muttered. "It's not as if I'm going to put you in a pie, Mrs Blackbird."

She shook her head and carried on walking. When she reached a fork in the path she stopped. Which way was it from here? Last year, had she turned left or right?

There was no recollection in her memory, so she shrugged and took the left path. She was left-handed, another thing that annoyed her mother, so she'd most likely taken that route.

Broad pawprints with distinct claws crossed the track. Badgers were around. She'd seen one once, when she'd been out walking with her father, but that was a long time ago.

Continuing and scanning the leafy forest floor for flora, she stepped over a small fallen log, then through a patch of sunlight streaming down from the canopy. Here, she paused.

A woodpecker tapped loudly overhead, marking his territory. And a plume of midges danced in the light, twirling and waltzing and spiralling up and down. Beyond the beams of finger-thin sunshine, something sparkled.

Water—a small lake or big pond.

The path veered towards it and so did she, drawn to the coolness. A stony bank held another log, rotting at one end and beached at an angle. "So I didn't go left before." If she had, she'd have remembered this pretty spot.

Sitting, she set her paints to one side and toed off her shoes. Next she lifted her gown to her thighs and carefully rolled down first her right, then her left stocking. She set them on her paints. Finally came her gloves, which she added atop her stockings.

For a moment she watched the fish, dainty little minnows, flashing as they darted through the clear water. Then she stood, raised her gown knee-high, and dipped her left toe into the cool water.

"Oh!" She laughed. It felt good.

A few more steps and she was ankle-deep. She sighed, then closed her eyes and lifted her face to the sunshine.

Suddenly she felt lighter, freer, as if the morning of advice and concern hadn't happened. The woodland lake was washing it away. She was still young, there was plenty of time to find a husband, and one she loved at that. Her mother's choices, which had been offered forward for several years now, were wholly unsuitable. Boring at best, creepy at worst, or completely unavailable, in their hearts if not on paper.

"Hey, little fishes," she said, looking down again. Her feet were blurry and pale on the lakebed; a tiny bit of green weed drifted past her big toe. She stared at it, wishing to paint its ribboned shape, but soon it went past.

Around the edge of the lake—about the size of a tennis lawn but with squashed curved corners—red oaks, sweet chestnuts, and beeches were heavy with leaves and lichen. Many had misshapen trunks with fissured bark indicating they were older than any human. Four large boulders, the shape and colour of big potatoes, sat on the opposite bank, and atop the biggest rock a jay eyed her warily.

She stilled completely, not wanting to scare it away until she'd admired its dusky-pink plumage complete with startling blue stripe on its wings. It held something in its beak, a berry or seed of some description.

A splash to her right. She turned to watch the ripples. A small fish likely had leapt to catch a fly.

The jay took to the air, and with a flash of blue, it was gone. But still, it had been a treat to see it. She wondered what else she might discover on her walk today.

* * * *

Thomas Kilead, Duke of Farrington, held his favourite feathered fountain pen poised over a blank sheet of paper and stared at the young woman who had just appeared from the thickness of the forest. She stood on the pebbled bank, clutching something in gloved hands, and studied the water.

He sat deathly still in the shadows of an oak tree, not wanting to be seen. He'd travelled from the Highlands, after all, to enjoy quiet time alone. For the last month, he'd had exactly that, but now...now an almost nymph-like creature had appeared as if from thin air and she stood slightly hazed by a thin strip of mist that loitered over the water.

Was he dreaming? Had solitude and isolation, being slave to his thoughts, pen, and words turned him quite mad?

He frowned and ignored a midge that was pestering him. What was she doing? What was she going to do?

Seeming to make a sudden decision, she sat on the log he'd used himself a few days ago, and set down her small cargo. With a flick of her right then her left foot, her shoes landed on the stones, one upside down, toe pointing at the water's edge.

A swallow skimmed the surface of the water, taking a drink on the wing. She didn't seem to notice for she had raised her gown above her knees and exposed her stockings.

Damn it.

What was he doing sitting here watching? He had to make himself known. It was the proper thing to do.

But he didn't, because the moment came and went, and now she was rolling her left stocking down her leg, exposing creamy flesh, long shapely calves, and slender ankles.

His breaths were shallow. A sense of misdeed gripped him. But how had *he* done anything wrong? He'd been minding his own business and waiting for inspiration to grip him.

It was *she* who had disturbed *him*.

The next stocking was slipped down, peeling from her slim ankle before being wafted in a shaft of sunlight and laid next to the first. The material was so sheer and diaphanous, a fairy's wing.

He swallowed. His throat was tight. It had been so long since he'd enjoyed the feel of a woman's soft flesh next to his. Too long. Maybe that was why he was spellbound.

A small thrill captured him when she stood, her gown held at her knees, and took a step to the water. She was going to paddle, he was sure of it.

He swallowed and wriggled his toes in his boots, imagining the press of the small stones on the fragile soles of her feet. She reached the lake and dipped one toe in, a gesture as graceful as any dancer.

"Oh!"

Her sweet exclamation rippled towards him.

Then she stepped deeper, up to her ankles. Her expression, from what he could make out, was one of sheer bliss—face lifted to the sun, eyes closed, long golden hair hanging down her back. She'd be enjoying the cool on the hot day, he'd done the same yesterday, except he'd stripped off completely and taken a swim.

*Will she do that?*

A part of him longed for her to remove her gown, swim the way he had, but the gentleman in him, the esteemed duke, knew that would make the situation even more improper. Hell, it would be downright sinful to watch from the shadows.

Fortunately, it seemed ankles were all she intended to wet. For a few moments she watched the fish, then her attention was caught by a jay on the boulders. It soon flew away with a shriek of indignation. And then she sat back on the log with her feet out in front of her, gown set on her shins, drying her delicate flesh.

There was something about her that was so peaceful and unguarded. It was as if he were seeing the real her. She sat quietly, gazing up at the birds, then appeared utterly captivated by a dragonfly that landed on her pale-lemon dress and stayed for several minutes.

He began to write, not a poem, just words so that he could fashion them into something meaningful later.

*Beauty. Magic. Grace. Spellbound. Ethereal. Silk. Butterfly. Birdsong. Sunlight. Golden. Fairy. Wisp. Willow. Delicate.*

For the first time in three days he was gripped by inspiration, his mind spouting words and ideas faster than he could write them down. He redipped his ink several times, though there was not much left in the well.

*Exquisite. Elegance. Creature. Fragile. Sprite. Summer. Isolation. Desire. Peace. Love.*

Damn and blast.

His inkwell had dried. He'd have to go back to the lodge and continue there. How remiss of him not to have enough. Frustrating, too.

Clutching his notepad to his chest, for the words were precious, he carefully eased backwards in a half crawl, half stoop. He was careful not to knock any branches with his head or shoulders as he eased away from the lake.

But when he stood straight, he stepped on a twig.

*Snap.*

He froze.

Through the foliage he could just see her.

She looked his way, directly. "Is anyone there?"

He crouched, his heart thumping. Turned his face away so the white of his skin wouldn't be visible. It would be impossible to explain him being there, watching her. She was clearly an elegant young lady, a debutante maybe, and the scandal of being watched refreshing herself in a lake could cause quite the upset if she were faint of heart.

"Hello?" she called.

He bit on his bottom lip, counted to sixty, and when she said no more, he resumed his stealthy departure. This time watching out for rogue twigs.

The track to Pheasant Lodge, property of his good friend Baron Gerald Millbank, was easy to follow if a little overgrown with nettles. More words kept filling his mind, and the ones he had he began to string together. It was the seeds of a new poem, a poem about the graceful nymph he'd seen by the water that day.

A deer hopped over the path in front of him. Usually he'd pause to admire it, search the woodland for more, but not today. He was in a hurry.

Thankfully, the lodge soon came into view, and he banged his notebook and pen onto the wooden table outside and rushed through the open door for more ink. He didn't need to close the door, certainly not lock it, he hadn't seen another soul in the month he'd been there.

Except for her.

And now she filled his mind, he had to get the emotions she'd evoked down on paper. Even if it took him all day and all night, he would make sure his poetry did her justice.

# Chapter Two

Elizabeth frowned at the dark shadows on the far side of the lake. Had someone been watching her? It hadn't felt like it, but then she never felt truly alone in the forest. There were so many creatures, big and small, insects and birds, too. Life was all around.

But she was sure she'd heard a twig snap as though it had been trodden on by something heavy. Perhaps it was a deer creeping around, waiting for her to leave so it could sneak down to the water's edge for a drink. There was no way of knowing.

Standing, stockings and shoes in place once more, she paused to watch a swallow take a beak full of water on the wing—a juvenile was close behind as if learning from its parent—then she turned back to the track.

She'd been out for at least an hour and hadn't painted a thing. Perhaps she'd get lucky with the anemone if she carried on this way.

After navigating around a patch of nettles she continued, glad of the cool shade after sitting in the sunshine. Her gloves, paints, and paper were hugged against her chest, and with her free hand she pushed soft greenstick branches and sharp brambles out of the way.

"Ah, there you are." In the distance a deer was staring straight at her, big brown eyes unblinking. "You can go and get your drink now."

She carried on walking, past a clump of garlic that fragranced the air and an anthill towering from the greenery. After turning to the right, the path opened up, and before her was a building.

It was single-storey with a thatched roof curving over two lead-paned windows and a heavy thatched porch sheltering an open door. A big bay window to the right had every window wide to the slight breeze. Pink roses crawled over the porch, and with the sun reaching through the clearing, it almost glowed. It had an impressive brick chimney on the wall to the left.

Compelled to study it more, she drew closer. It wasn't until she was almost upon it did she notice a man stooped over a table beside what had been an outdoor fire but was now a heap of ash. He appeared deep in concentration with his quill to paper, an inkwell at his side.

She stopped. Stared. She should announce herself, but it was as if a spell had been cast over him, such was his absorption. He was writing frantically. On the table were several pieces of screwed-up paper, discarded, as though full of errors and thrown in frustration.

Perhaps she shouldn't disturb him at all, just continue on her way. Although which way she wasn't so sure, she was beginning to feel quite lost. Had she wandered onto Millbank land?

Stepping carefully, she made her way past the lodge, trying not to look at a string of dead rabbits and pheasants hanging from a wire.

But as soon as she drew level with him, not ten feet away, he raised his head.

"You!" he said, quill poised in the air like a pointing finger. He frowned, two neat lines creasing his brow. His blond hair had amber streaks running through it, and his skin was tan, as though he spent a lot of time outdoors.

Her heart skipped a beat at the sudden loud volume of his voice. "Oh, er, I'm sorry to disturb you." She nearly dropped her paints and clasped them tighter, rearranging her grip.

"What are you doing here?" he asked in a heavily accented voice.

"I'm just passing." She pointed to the track ahead.

"Passing to where?"

"I...are you from Scotland?"

"Aye?" He set down his pen. "Passing to where, I asked you? The only place yonder is The Millbank Estate."

"Oh." So she had come too far.

"You'll be wanting the village?" He raised his eyebrows.

"Er, yes, I would." At least if she got to Littlemead she'd be able to get her bearings and walk home from there, even if it was a bit of a trek.

"You need to go that way." He pointed his quill to her right.

A narrow track wound through a copse of pine trees.

"Will take just less than an hour," he said, "stream's fair dry, so crossing it is easy."

"Oh, I see. Thank you." She paused. "Are you the new gamekeeper for The Millbank Estate?"

"What do you think?"

Elizabeth didn't know. That was why she'd asked. Broad-shouldered and with big hands, he certainly appeared strong enough, and his jawline was coated in stubble, darker than his hair, as though shaving wasn't something he did often.

"I think you are, and I will leave you to your...writing."

He kind of huffed then ducked his head again and dipped his quill in ink.

Rude.

She took one last look at the pretty gamekeeper's lodge then took the path towards the pines.

Three hours later, Elizabeth arrived home weary and hungry.

"Elizabeth, where have you been?" her mother fussed when she caught her having a tray of sandwiches delivered to her room.

"I went to the forest, to paint."

"What have I told you about wandering off?" She frowned and put her hands on her hips. The grey curled strands of hair around her face bobbed.

"I'm perfectly safe. There's no one there, and if I want to paint woodland flowers, I have to go to the forest."

No one there? That wasn't quite true. An image of the gamekeeper came to mind. Was it usual for gamekeepers to write? She didn't know. Perhaps he was still learning, hence the discarded paper.

"Well, if you do come across someone, likely they will be up to no good." She clicked her tongue on the roof of her mouth like an angry hen. "I don't know why you can't just paint the flowers in the garden, heaven knows there's plenty of them."

"I've already studied them." She reached for a cucumber sandwich. "You know I'm trying to capture the image of every flower that grows wild in Hertfordshire. A catalogue of sorts."

"You have more important things to think about, young lady."

"Like finding a husband." She huffed.

"Yes. Exactly that." Her mother shook her head and walked to the window, stared out at the sweeping driveway that led past the huge lake complete with tumbling waterfall designed by Lancelot Capability Brown for Elizabeth's grandfather. "In fact," she said, "perhaps I should throw a summer ball, invite all of the eligible young men from miles around. Yes, when your father and I return from London next week, I will start preparations."

"Please, no, not another ball, I—"

"It is the perfect way for you to meet someone suitable. You can fill your dance card and then make a decision. Yes. I'm sure your father will agree, this spinster lifestyle of yours has gone on quite long enough."

"I don't think it's something that should be rushed, deciding who to marry. Who to spend your life with."

"Every other debutante of your year is wed, many have given their new husbands heirs, too."

"Huh, is that my only role? To have babies?" She pointed at her paintings. They were all carefully labelled and filed, and soon she'd compile them into one volume and take it to London in search of a publisher. "I'm sure God would have me do more with my life."

"Like scribbling with your paints. I don't think so."

"Like recording the nature He has gifted us on Earth."

Her mother turned and raised her hands. "I am not going to argue about this with you. When you are wed it will be your husband's problem, not mine, this obsession with getting a book into print with your paintings and notes has gone too far."

"I will only take a husband who doesn't think my ambition is a problem." Her voice was getting louder, but she couldn't help it. The thought of the frantic preparations before a ball and her mother's dismissive attitude about her work was guaranteed to stoke her anger.

Her mother pursed her lips and clenched her fists. She then blew out a breath. "Dinner at seven, don't spoil your appetite." And with that, she left the room.

Elizabeth ate another sandwich, then set about washing her paintbrushes. She had found woodland anemone to paint and was pleased with the result.

Her heart suddenly sank. "Oh, how annoying." One of her gloves was missing. They'd been a gift from her late grandmother. She must have dropped it when she was out walking, but it could be anywhere along the trail, beside the lake, back towards the village. Retracing her steps would take an entire afternoon.

But her parents were taking a trip to London, so if she spent a day walking with her paints and searching for her glove, she might just find it. She might also find deadly belladonna, an elusive and toxic purple flowering plant she had yet to add to her collection.

Pausing, she went to the window and stood in the spot her mother just had. She knew her mother was frustrated that she didn't have a son-in-law yet, no grandchildren, but Elizabeth couldn't marry just to keep her mother happy. She wanted a husband who had wit and charm and was interesting to be around. Someone kind and patient who understood her and didn't dismiss anything she did as merely 'time-wasting women's stuff'—an expression she'd heard her father use.

Was a husband like that too much to ask for?

The next morning, she stood at the grand entrance to the Burghley home and bid her parents farewell.

"We will see you in one week from this day, Beth," her father said, kissing her on both cheeks.

"Enjoy yourselves." She liked it when he called her Beth, it meant he was in a good mood. He was clearly looking forward to his trip to London.

"We have a full diary of engagements." Her mother held Elizabeth's shoulders and also kissed her cheeks. "Is there anything you would like bringing back from the ton?"

"Yes, please, a quire of laid paper."

"More paper?" Her father turned and raised his golden-tipped cane. "My dear, you will bankrupt us with your need for paper."

"It is just my paintings are coming along so well and—"

He laughed. "Of course we will bring you paper, a young lady needs to be entertained." He bobbed his head then got into the ruby-red coach that stood waiting behind four bay horses.

"No, no," her mother said to one of the footmen. "Put that basket in with us, it is such a long way, we will need refreshments."

"Yes, my lady."

"Farewell, dear," her mother said with a smile. "Until we return."

Elizabeth watched them disappear down the long, tree-lined drive—her lady's maid, Sarah, waiting a step behind her—then she turned and went back into the house.

"Would you like me to bring you anything?" Sarah asked.

"No, thank you. I have paintings to organise, and I will take supper in my room, as I am the only person in residence."

"Very good, my lady." Sarah dipped her knees then disappeared.

Just before noon the next day, Elizabeth slipped out of the side entrance with her paper, paints, and brushes stowed in a leather bag. It was once again a warm day, and she'd opted for a pale-pink gown that brushed the tops of her ankles. But the forest was cool, so she'd thrown a white shawl around her shoulders that matched her bonnet.

Passing the old elm tree she'd climbed as a child with her cousins, she had a distinct sense of anticipation. It coiled in her stomach, fizzed a little, too. Was it the thought of finding the glove, deadly nightshade, or was it seeing the surly gamekeeper again?

There was no denying she'd thought about him since their brief meeting. It was almost as if he were from another world. Hunched at his rough-edged table, scribbling. Dead animals hanging by their feet and necks. A small lodge with only one door and one chimney. It was so far from what she was used to. All her life she'd lived with grandeur, priceless antiques, never a concern as to money or food or rent. What must it be like to have to hunt for your dinner? To have to chop wood to keep warm in the winter? Live alone, no maids, servants, cooks?

Was it all of those things that made him gruff? Because yes, he had been ill-tempered.

But even so, he'd intrigued her.

She kept her eyes on the ground, searching for her lost white glove, and when she reached the woodland, flowers, too.

After an hour of walking and still nothing, she stopped and took her bonnet off, caught the stray hairs, and smoothed them to her head. She was glad of the rest; once more it was a warm summer's day. But she didn't linger for long, because it felt like she had purpose, she wasn't simply wandering.

After passing the lake, and the spot she'd seen the deer the day before, she arrived at the lodge.

Today a dribble of smoke trickled from the chimney, and the windows were closed. Two more rabbits had been added to the wire, and a brown jug sat on the table.

She glanced around, wondering where the gamekeeper was. A jacket was roughly laid on a wooden stool and an axe speared into a splitting log.

A flash of white caught her attention. Her glove. It was stuck atop a long stick as if it were waving at her.

So this was where she'd dropped it. Typical.

She walked over to it. She didn't have many things that were senti-mental, but her grandmother's gloves were exactly that.

While plucking it from the stick, there was movement at the lodge door.

A figure appeared.

A man.

He was naked from the waist up, and his buckskin breeches hung low on his lean hips—a trail of light-brown hair led from his navel to the waistband.

*Oh dear Lord.*

Quickly, she averted her eyes and clasped the glove.

"You found it then," he said.

"I...yes, thank you." She dared a glance at him.

"Good." He strolled over to the axe and drew it from the stump it was speared into. "You know your way back to the village now, am I right?"

"I do. But I had to retrace my steps today for I really didn't want to lose a glove. This glove in particular."

He kind of huffed and reached for a log to split. The muscles in his back and shoulders rippled, and his biceps bulged as he set it on its end.

Unable to tear her eyes away, Elizabeth watched him raise the axe, his torso stretching, then bring it down with a loud crack. The log split.

He set his attention on her. "Are you waiting for tea and cake? Be-cause if that is the case, I don't have any."

"I...no, of course not." She paused. "You don't have any tea or you don't have any cake?"

"Do I look like a cook? A pastry chef?"

"No, not really."

He reached for another log.

"But I wish to thank you, you could have thrown the glove away but you did not. What is your name?"

"Why do you want to know?"

"It is polite when giving thanks to use a person's name."

He stared at her for a moment, then, "Tom."

"Thank you, Tom. I appreciate your guardianship of my late grandmother's glove."

Once again his brow creased. "What's your name?"

"Elizabeth."

"You're welcome, Beth." He turned, signifying an end to their conversation, so she didn't bother to correct him. He'd obviously misheard her name. All that splitting logs had likely made him hard of hearing.

The axe was raised, his body tense, then he brought it down with a thunderous crack. The log fell in two pieces to the ground.

He repeated the action, the sheen of sweat between his shoulder blades catching the sunlight.

Elizabeth swallowed, knowing she was staring but unable to help herself. He was beautiful in a masculine, powerful, earthy way. Raw muscle, at one with the land, almost feral.

A strange sensation gripped her belly. Admiration, longing, fascination.

"There'll be rain soon," he said gruffly. "Best run along."

"What? Oh, yes, of course." He'd made her feel like a silly young girl which irked her. "Good day to you, Tom." She turned and hurried towards the copse of pine trees.

Her cheeks flushed, and her heart rate picked up. He must have known she'd been watching him. But it was hardly her fault. She'd never seen a man like him, and not just that, a man like him wearing so little. Who could blame her for being affected by the sight of him?

# Chapter Three

"Sarah, tell Cook to make a honey cake." Elizabeth strode through the front door of Burghley House.

"Yes, my lady. Of course." Sarah took Elizabeth's shawl and bonnet from her.

"And that she has to be sure to make it the best she has ever made. Then when it is cooled, wrap it in paper and string, for I wish to take it somewhere tomorrow."

"You do?" Sarah's eyebrows rose.

"Yes." Elizabeth pressed her lips together and climbed the sweeping staircase, holding her gown up a few inches. She had no intention of divulging to Sarah the idea she'd come up with on the way home from the forest.

With every step from the gamekeeper's lodge, she'd grown more sorry that she wouldn't see Tom again. Not that he was particularly cordial with her, just that he intrigued her. His way of life, his skills...his strong body, so different to hers, were all captivating.

So she'd come up with a plan to take him a cake the next day to say thank you for placing her glove on a stick and making it easy for her to find. He said he had no cake and wasn't a chef. And Cook's honey cake was the best, a recipe handed down for generations and kept very secret. So if she took him cake, not just a slice but the entire thing, he was sure to be happy.

Although whether or not he ever smiled, she wasn't so sure.

She entered her room and flopped backwards onto the bed, arms spread wide, and stared up at the embroidered canopy. If only Tom was one of the handsome suitors her mother kept introducing her to. Perhaps then she'd have some interest. He'd sparked something in her no other gentleman had managed to.

19

When she closed her eyes she could see his back view. The gutter of his spine, the indents of his muscles, the way his breeches hung on his buttocks.

"Oh, I'll burn in Hell," she muttered, flipping onto her stomach and burying her face in the soft covers.

The next day couldn't come soon enough. Thank goodness her parents weren't at home.

The cake had smelled divine on Elizabeth's entire walk through the forest, the scent seeping out of the brown paper. She'd held it against her dress and hoped none of the moisture would leak through. It was one of her favourite daytime gowns. Bought in London, it was deep red with black lace at the neckline, cuffs, and hem. She'd added a matching shawl, as like yesterday there were a few menacing clouds threatening to drench everything and everyone below.

Just before the lodge came into view she stopped, took a deep breath, and grasped the cake and adjusted the shoulder strap of her bag.

Oh, but what was she doing? This was absurd. Certainly not the way a titled young lady should be behaving. It was practically scandalous.

A wave of shame washed through her, mean and spiky. The cake was way overboard as a thank you for picking up a glove. She'd look a fool. She *was* a fool.

"You're here... again?"

"Oh!" She spun around, her bones seeming to jump within her skin.

"You're here again," Tom repeated as he pushed a lock of hair from his face. He was fully dressed today and held a notebook and a quill. He still hadn't shaved, and his jawline was even heavier with facial hair.

"Yes, it's not far for me to come and..." She held the cake forward. "I brought you this."

"What is it?" He made no move to take it.

"Cake. Honey cake. The absolute best, I can assure you, and made from fine ingredients. You won't taste another like it in your life."

"Really?" He cocked his head to one side, studying her.

"Yes. Really." She shifted from one foot to the other, feeling as foolish and tongue-tied as she'd known she would.

"Did you bake it?"

"What? I, er...no."

"So who did? How do you know it is made of the finest ingredients?"

"It is, and...and...a friend."

"A good friend, I would say. It appears heavy." Finally, he took it. "It *is* heavy."

"It should last you several days, which is good, living all the way out here and you not being a chef. I mean, it's a hard profession, I'm sure, and just as hard to source the flour, honey, eggs, sugar when you're living in the forest, so I thought you would enjoy it, and I wanted to say thank you again for finding my glove and..." She knew she was rambling. "And I was out this way anyway, looking for woodland plants and—"

"Looking for woodland plants?"

"Yes." She took a breath and closed her eyes in a long blink. *Calm down.* "I paint them. I've been working my way through everything in this area and building a catalogue."

"And what will you do with this catalogue?"

"I should like to get it published. In London. Perhaps have it stored in libraries for reference."

"You have mighty ambitions, Beth."

"It would have seemed a mighty ambition to start with, but now I have a detailed drawing and description of all but a few of the flora in the forest and meadow yonder."

"That must have taken a very long time."

"Two years now." She frowned. "A few are still eluding me, though, and I know they are in the forest because I've seen them before. Perhaps the weather conditions haven't been right this year. Or maybe the deer or rabbits have eaten the shoots." She shrugged. "It's hard to know, but it's disappointing."

"What are you looking for, if I might ask?"

"Belladonna for one, tall with purple bell-shaped flowers and then dark berries come autumn."

"You missed out an important detail about belladonna."

"I did?"

"Aye, it's highly poisonous."

"That is true. I think the villagers might have pulled it up in the Littlemead area to stop the children playing near it or eating the berries by mistake, but there should be some this deep into the forest."

"You'd be right."

"I beg your pardon."

"You'd be right. Follow me."

"Follow you? But I...?"

He stepped around her and began walking to the cottage, his long legs eating the ground and his booted footsteps silent on the soft earth.

She stared after him for a moment and then quickly followed.

But he didn't go into the cottage. Instead, he walked to the left, past the big window and a stack of chopped logs. He kept on going and went out of view.

She continued to follow, and as she, too, turned the corner, she nearly bumped into him. "Oh."

He didn't seem to notice her sudden halt. "There. Is that what you need?"

"My goodness, you have belladonna growing right here." She leaned closer. "And it's in full bloom. Absolutely perfect for painting this very day."

"This very day?" He placed his hands on his hips. "Like...now."

"Yes, now. See how the petals have unfurled and the stamen is in full view, the pollen thick. This is exactly how I must capture it." She glanced around. "Do you have a chair of some description?"

"You want a chair?" He appeared confused.

"A lady can't sit on the earth in a gown." She laughed, feeling light and excited at the prospect of painting. "A chair if you please."

He kind of huffed. "Coming right up, Your Majesty."

"Oh, but..." She drew out a sheet of paper. "Don't be silly. I'm hardly a queen."

He didn't reply before he disappeared. A few moments later, he returned with a low milking stool. "Will this suffice?"

"Yes, thank you." She took it and set her behind on the small round seat.

Within a few minutes she was all set, and the lighting was perfect. There'd be no excuse to not get a great painting of the pretty but deadly plant.

"Anything else I can get you?"

"No, that will be all." She selected a brush and dipped it in a tiny pot of water.

She was aware of his presence behind her, his shadow stretching over the belladonna. "I...er...do you mind?"

"What?"

She flicked her wrist at the weedy patch of earth. "Your shadow, it's on the plant. It's affecting the way the light falls."

He stepped back. "Pardon me for breathing," he muttered.

"Oh, but..." She spun around, but he was already out of view and out of earshot.

She sighed. Perhaps she had been a little presumptuous to think he wouldn't mind her sitting painting outside his home. But she hadn't been able to help it. It was the artist in her.

Soon her thoughts were a hundred miles from Tom, her parents, Burghley House, and she was lost to the paint. It was a tricky task to find exactly the right shades of purple and lilac for the petals, and the delicate stamen.

A cuckoo called behind her, and a rustle as a pile of leaves were disturbed to her left. A fox or rabbit perhaps. But she didn't waver from her concentration. She had to get this exactly right, so that if someone held her picture in their hand and came across belladonna without knowing what it was, they'd be able to identify it.

All the more important with something so imbued with poison.

Eventually, she finished and was happy with the result. The sun had dipped, though it was still early afternoon. The trees around the lodge kept the area shrouded in shadow for all but highest hour. She'd been lucky to have arrived when she had.

Setting her painting to one side, she stowed her things away, poured the water onto the grass, and stood. Then with her picture in one hand, bag hoisted over her shoulder, and the stool in the other hand, she walked back to the front of the cottage.

Would Tom still be home? Or had he gone out hunting, trap laying, or whatever it was a gamekeeper spent his days doing?

The front door to the cottage was open, and the ashy scent of smoke reached her. Judging by a herby, meaty smell, she guessed a meal was being prepared.

"Good day," she called.

Suddenly, Tom's face appeared from the gloom of the cottage. "Hardly." He tutted. "I've made no progress with my work, but perhaps you've had success with yours."

"Yes, thank you. It was a beautiful specimen."

He raised his eyebrows. "So can I look, or are you one of those irritating artists who hate to show their work?"

"I...of course...are some artists really like that?" She handed him the painting.

He took it and studied it. "Perhaps only the ones who are truly terrible at their craft."

"You think that's truly terrible?" Her heart sank. Her parents had told her she was gifted, as had two of her governesses. Had they all just been humouring her?

"On the contrary," he said, peering closer. "It's quite...exquisite. You're really very capable."

"Oh, why thank you." She pulled in a deep breath, the dark pit of disillusionment retreating. "I do enjoy it very much and hope my paintings will be helpful to someone, one day."

"I'm sure they will be." He handed the painting back and stepped deeper into the cottage. "I'm going to try the cake. Would you like to join me in a slice?"

The truth was her stomach had rumbled twice in the last hour. "Yes please, if you don't mind."

"I don't have tea," he called over his shoulder, "only wine."

"Wine?"

"Aye." Pause. "Well, come in then."

She stepped over the threshold and waited a moment for her eyes to adjust.

The cottage was larger inside than she'd expected with a narrow staircase to her right. Next to it was a large hob grate, a fire flickering within it, and beyond that a long counter piled high with jars of pickles, a basket of vegetables, a stack of eggs that appeared somewhat precarious, and several bottles. Beside it a box of dusty potatoes and a sack tied with a length of fraying rope.

A table sat before the fire, cluttered with paper and quills and inkwells and a tower of books that appeared as perilous as the eggs. Nearer to where she stood were two worn seats with faded cushions; they each seemed to hold the shape of the last person to sit in them. A rug, made of fur, stretched out on the floor between them, and a squat oak table, dusty, was positioned at one end.

"Please, sit." He gestured to the chair nearest her.

"Thank you." She sat, placed her bag on the floor beside her feet, and smoothed her gown.

"I beg your forgiveness for the dust," he said, handing her a goblet of wine. "I wasn't expecting company."

"I'm sorry to disturb you."

He let out a sigh. It wasn't quite frustration but it was far from relaxed. "Perhaps it will do me good to get out of my own head for a while."

"What do you mean?"

He walked to the table, picked up a plate and another goblet, then sat opposite her.

Curiosity was making her itch, but she forced herself to remain quiet. What she really wanted was to get him to tell her everything about himself. Including did he have a wife? Children? Did he care not that he'd been wearing so little when she'd come across him the day before? And was any part of him grateful that she'd brought him cake?

# Chapter Four

Thomas sat, crossed his ankles, and settled back into his new favourite armchair. It wasn't a Sheraton, which he was used to, but it had a nice lived-in feel to it. The cushions were soft and yielding, and he could think for hours at a time, stringing his poems together in his mind, or at least trying to.

His stay at Pheasant Lodge wasn't turning out to be as productive as he'd hoped. While his houseguest here appeared to be romping along with her artist project, his had barely got off the ground.

He took a sip of wine, hoping to wash away the frustration.

She mimicked him. "Oh!" She licked her lips, the pink tip of her tongue peeking out. "I have to say this is very good claret."

"Did you not expect it to be?" He raised his chin.

"Well, I..."

And then he realised what she saw—a fellow with four days' beard growth, hair that hadn't been brushed that morn, and wearing clothes that hadn't been laundered since he'd left Scotland. Naturally, she didn't expect him to be any kind of wine connoisseur. He lived a rough life in the forest, splitting wood and hunting his dinner.

"I have a fondness for Burgundy wine, not easy to come across these days, but I indulge myself when I do."

"In that case, thank you for sharing it with me." She took another sip and sat back a little, adjusted the cushion at her right arm. "It will go well with the cake."

"Aye. Of course. Help yourself." He gestured to the small table that held the cake.

"Thank you." She took a piece.

He watched her eat. She really was as delicate and graceful as he'd remembered. That first time he'd seen her he'd been quite captivated, almost spellbound. He could have been fooled that his imagination had dreamed her up to be his muse.

But she wasn't a dream.

She was sitting in Pheasant Lodge with wine and cake and looking around as though she'd never been inside a place so humble.

"So are you going to tell me?" she asked after a moment.

"Tell you what?"

"Why you need to get out of your own head?"

He sighed. "I guess if anyone would understand it would be you, since you also are a creator."

She raised her eyebrows. "I will certainly try to understand."

He considered her for a moment. Did he believe her? Actually, aye, he did. There was a flash of earnestness in her eyes, intelligence, too. And he liked that...a lot.

"Are you trying to learn to write?" she asked.

"*Learn* to write?" He was shocked by the suggestion.

"Yes. When I came by the first time you were sat with paper and quill surrounded by discarded paper. I guessed you were finding it harder to write than you'd hoped." She paused. "I can help if you'd like. I'm quite proficient."

Thomas didn't know which was more insulting, that she thought he couldn't write or that she, a village girl, could instruct him in learning. "I...I can write perfectly well I'll have you know."

"Oh, well, that's good." She took another sip of wine. "It's a great skill to have."

"Aye. Most useful." He reached for his slice of cake and chomped into it, barely tasting it, such was his vexation in what he was about to say. "My problem is poetry. Or rather lack of it." He brushed at a crumb sitting on his shirt.

"Poetry." Her eyes widened. "You write poetry?"

"Do not be so surprised, Beth. It was good enough for Chaucer, Byron, Burns, why not me?"

"I totally agree. Why not you?" She leaned forward and blinked. Twisted her lips as though thinking.

He couldn't help but notice her long lashes and the smoothness of her skin.

"It's really not something I'm very good at, poetry, that is," she said. "Despite a few attempts."

"It's just a case of digging deep."

"I don't understand."

"Poetry is the quiet voice at the very back of your mind." He tapped the crown of his head.

She nodded slowly.

He went on. "It's the place where truth exists and lies shrivel and die. It's the very essence of emotion and can bring tears and joy and anger and passion with only a few sentences."

"You describe it beautifully, and that is certainly my experience of reading poetry. Are you just starting out, or has this been an ambition for a while?"

For some reason her interest was a relief. It validated him being here in England. "I've been producing poetry for a few years." He had to stop himself from telling her he'd had a volume published by Castle Cawl Press and was being pestered for the second because it had been so popular. He'd pushed it with Beth in being a gamekeeper who enjoyed fine claret. Being a published poet on top of that and she'd be asking more questions than about his poems.

"And do you have anything you'd be willing to share with me?" she asked.

"Not at present." He forced a smile. "But I'm working on something, and it's taking shape quite..." He watched her check her lips with the tip of her finger for crumbs. "Really quite beautifully."

"Then I am thrilled for you. Truly." She beamed.

He smiled, too, and let his attention slip from her pretty face, over the rise of her bosoms to her scarlet dress. He'd like to have her sit there while he wrote. Capture every verb and emotion she produced in him and likely in every other man she met. Protectiveness. Curiosity. Desire.

Awe. There were so many, and they rushed and swirled even as he sat still. Just like the other day at the lake.

"Have you lived here long?" she asked.

"No, I only arrived last month."

"And you are finding Baron Millbank to be a fair employer?"

"Employer? Er, aye, I suppose he is a congenial fellow."

"That is good."

"Have you heard otherwise?" He was curious now as to what the villagers thought of their neighbour and landlord.

"Not at all. I've always heard that he is very much the gentleman." She nodded at the door. "Do you get much trouble with poachers here? Does that get regular use?"

"The rifle? No, the land is well enclosed in the majority with hedgerows and thickets which are a clear sign not to enter. I've been told the pheasant population took a severe hit, but the enclosure act has helped with that and keeping Gerald...I mean Baron Millbank's stock, safe. I hope not to have to use the gun, at least not on poachers." He really wasn't sure he was cut out for that.

"Gerald," she repeated. "Are you and he—?"

"I'm incredibly grateful to him. Would you like to hear a poem about pheasants?"

"Yes. Very much so." She leaned back and took a sip of wine then smiled at him over the rim.

He pulled in a deep breath, closed his eyes, and hoped to remember the words.

"The whirring pheasant springs. And mounts, exulting on triumphant wings: Ah! What avails his glossy, varying dyes. His purple crest, and scarlet-circled eyes. The vivid green his shining plumes unfold. His painted wings, and breast that flames with gold." He let the images hang in the air between them.

"Oh my goodness." She sighed and pressed her hand to her chest, where her heart might be. "That is beautiful. You really are talented."

"Alas." He huffed. "They are not my words but that of Alexander Pope. I'm an admirer of his."

"I can see why." She set her wine to one side.

"Would you like more wine?"

"No, thank you. I will leave you to enjoy your fine claret and more cake should you feel the need."

"You were most kind to bring it. The sweetness was a rare treat."

She picked up her bag, stood, and gestured around. "Don't most gamekeepers own a dog or two?"

"I beg your pardon?"

"A dog? Don't you have one?"

"Ah, I see what you mean. Aye, it is rather unusual, isn't it?" He also stood and then felt as though he towered above her small frame. "I will rectify the situation shortly."

"You should, it would be most useful." She studied him quizzically for a moment, then retrieved her painting. "I will bid you farewell, Tom, and thank you for the wine and cake."

"Do not thank me for the cake, it was you who brought it."

She smiled and tightened her bonnet, then made her way to the open door. She stepped outside, a ray of sunlight slicing between two branches landing on her, seeming to guild her dress so that it shimmered as she moved.

"Beth," he called after her.

She turned.

"What other plants do you need to paint to complete your study?"

"Lady orchid, which is frustrating when it grows so tall yet I cannot find it."

"It stands to your height, and the flowers are deep red, almost purple, right?"

"Yes, but it is also delicious to deer, so although I've searched and searched, I'm struggling."

"Have you looked yonder? Beside the lake?"

"The lake? Oh yes, I know where the lake is."

"Just beyond it is a rocky cliff, as if some of the land has fallen away, I might be wrong, but I think I saw some tall purple flowers there. It's not a grazing site for deer."

"You did?"

He nodded. Swallowed. Hardly believing his next words were forming and about to be put out into the open. "I can show you if you'd like...sometime."

"Tomorrow?"

"Tomorrow. Well..."

"It's okay, if you're busy with..." She gestured around. "Tasks to perform. I'll find this rocky place by myself."

"No, no, it really is particularly steep. What if you were to fall?"

She smiled. "I'm sure I would be quite all right."

"I'll come with you, I insist. Your parents would never forgive me if I let you go alone."

"My parents?"

"Aye, you have parents, do you not?" Damn it. Had they died? Was she an orphan?

"Yes, yes, I have parents." She seemed to think about it for a moment. "Shall we meet at noon?"

"At the lake?"

"Yes." She nodded, "Now I really have taken up too much of your time. Have a good day, Tom." She turned and walked towards the track.

Dear Lord in Heaven, what had he done? So much for finding the solitude to write.

But then again, perhaps Beth had been sent to him for a reason. His mind was alive with poetry, or potential poetry, when she was around. There was something about her that inspired him. Held his attention hostage.

Maybe taking her to the lake was all part of God's rich plan for his next book.

\* \* \* \*

Elizabeth walked back to the Burghley Estate with a tingling sensation spreading from her stomach to her skin. It was pleasant, like being tickled with feathers. And every time she thought of Tom, a new wave captured her.

He was unlike any of the men her mother had introduced her to over the years. He was less polished, his emotions showed on his face, in his actions and words. If she were honest it was a relief. Manners were all well and good, but sometimes they were a mask to what someone was really thinking.

And Tom seemed to do a lot of thinking. About words and poems in particular. If she'd had to guess what his passion was when she'd first met him, she would never in a million years have said poetry. Lilting words and gentle rhymes just didn't match his gruff exterior. Oh, but when he'd recited Pope's poem in his Highland accent, speaking about pheasants and flames of gold, she'd been quite captivated and would have happily listened to more.

When she reached home she was hot and perspiring and her head swirling with thoughts of Tom and seeing him the next day.

"I have drawn you a jasmine bath," Sarah said, setting down a tea tray on Elizabeth's desk.

"Thank you. I will take it momentarily." She touched her hair. "Perhaps you would wash my hair for me, too."

"Of course. If we curl it overnight it will be ready for church on Sunday."

"Church on Sunday." Gosh, she was loosing track of time. That was the day after tomorrow.

"Will you want me to chaperone you? As your parents are in the ton?"

"I...er...yes, that is a good idea, Sarah." Elizabeth tucked her gloves in a drawer. "What would I do without you?" She smiled.

"I'm at your service, my lady. And grateful everyday to work for such a charming and kind family."

"I'm pleased you think that way." She sipped her tea. "Oh, and tell Cook the cake was delicious."

"I will do." She paused. "Can I ask who it was for?"

Elizabeth stared out of the window, looking over the grand lawns, lake, and to the forest beyond. "A friend."

Sarah was silent, knowing it wasn't appropriate to ask further questions.

"Can you set out my new blue dress, please?"

"For church. Of course."

"No...actually, I'm going to wear it tomorrow." Elizabeth didn't turn to see if there was a surprised expression on Sarah's face. "I'll wear my pink gown for church, the one with the butterfly embroidery."

"Very good, my lady."

Sarah busied herself at the vast mahogany wardrobe that stood on clawed brass feet.

After finishing her tea, Elizabeth wandered into the bathroom. A soak in warm fragrant water was a good idea. All of this walking through the forest was tiring.

# Chapter Five

Elizabeth arrived at the lake a little before noon. Standing at the water's edge, she searched for the jay she'd seen previously. There was no sign of it, but she spotted a robin, its breast pale as new feathers came in.

Once again, the dawn had brought a hot, brilliant sun and humid air, but clouds were building in the west, swollen-bellied and steely grey.

The summer was stretching on. Soon the harvest would be brought in. Farmers and farmhands so busy they'd be working under moonlight.

A small fish leapt from the water, then landed with a plop, winged bug in its mouth. She took a deep breath and was glad to have returned to such a pretty place. If she hadn't been so intent on her study of flora she'd have tried to capture the lake with trees tickling its banks and the canopy of leaves reflected in the inky surface like a wobbling mirror.

From where she stood there were no tall purple flowers to be seen, but the potato-shaped rocks opposite did suggest there was a cliffy bank nearby.

"Beth, you are here. I do hope I did not keep you waiting?"

She turned, her heart doing a strange little flip. "Tom. Good day. No, I have only just arrived." His boots were worn, but his buckskin breeches were clean, as was his white linen shirt, though it had come untucked on one side, giving him a bit of a roguish look. He'd also shaved, his smooth jawline square and with a tiny vertical dent in his chin that she hadn't noticed before.

"Good. I would have hated to inconvenience you." He held a notebook, inkwell, and quill.

"It is you who is inconvenienced. I am sure you have many gamekeeper tasks to attend."

"Nothing that cannot wait." He lifted the book. "I will take the opportunity to write while you paint."

"What an excellent idea. But first we must find this elusive flower."

"Aye. Come. This way." Before he turned, his gaze slid down her body, all the way to her feet and back up.

Heat attacked her cheeks. Did he like what he saw? She hoped so. This was her favourite dress, and it fitted her to perfection. Sarah had done a lovely job curling her hair. She hadn't worn a bonnet today, for she hadn't wanted to flatten it.

The truth couldn't be denied, she'd wanted to be pretty for Tom.

He pulled in a breath, walked past the rotting log that lay on the shingle, then took a path she hadn't noticed before.

She followed, lifting her gown so it didn't catch on brambles.

It was barely a track, and she had to duck a few times and climb over a lichen-dotted rock. At one point, Tom held back a particularly nasty clump of nettles so she could get past them without being stung.

"Not far now," he said, batting at a wasp.

"Good." She peered into the distance. "Oh! There they are."

He followed her line of sight. "That is them?"

"Yes, definitely, and beautiful specimens, too. I cannot thank you enough, they really have been quite taxing to find."

"I am pleased to be of assistance."

A couple of minutes later, the path mercifully widened and provided them with a rocky seating arrangement.

The lady's orchid were a few feet up the craggy slope, but Elizabeth had a good view of them and got straight to work.

Tom set his inkwell on a flat stone and opened his notepad.

Soon she was lost in her painting. Working hard to perfectly capture the shape of the stem, the curve of the fleshy leaves, and the rosette of flowers that sprang up, cone-like, the petals arranged in such a way they could be described as ladies' crinoline ball gowns.

A few times she paused and rolled her shoulders, tipped her head from left to right, and then continued.

The sound of Tom's quill gently scratching over the paper mixed with the murmurs of the woodland.

Eventually, she was happy with her finished result and she set the picture to dry and stood. "I do believe that is one of the last paintings I need." She laughed, feeling relieved. "Though, of course, there are more flowering plants all across the country."

"Scotland, too," he said, not glancing up from his writing. "Thistles, heather, and myrtle."

"That is true." She sighed. "Maybe one day I will be lucky enough to go."

"Would you like to?" He stopped writing and studied her.

"Yes. I've heard it is very beautiful."

"It is that. A hard life for some, though, the weather is not as moderate as here."

"That is also what I've heard." She glanced upward, through the gap in the trees. At that very moment, a threateningly dark cloud slid over the sun.

It was as if a dense woollen cloak had been thrown over the forest. The air chilled, and before she had time to comment, a blob of rain landed on her cheek.

"Quick," Tom said. "Gather your things. The heavens are going to open."

Elizabeth was already protecting her new painting. She slipped that and her paints away, and then wished she'd worn a bonnet and taken a shawl after all.

"To the lodge," Tom said, pressing his hand on the small of her back. "And as fast as you can."

"But..." She took a few swift steps onto the track.

"You have no time to get to the village before this downpour." Tom continued to urge her along. "We must get to shelter and ride out the—"

An enormous bellow of thunder drowned out his words, and the trunks around them lit with a white-hot flash of lightning.

"Oh dear Lord," she gasped. Tom was right. They had to get to shelter fast.

They hurried past the nettles, not being as careful as before, and she felt the prickle of stings on her right ankle. She ducked beneath a branch, almost leapt the brambles' arms, and then broke into a run. Tom was rushing along behind her when they reached the track at the lake.

By the time the lodge came into view it was raining hard. A torrential wall that slapped onto the leaves and plopped onto the baked earth.

She was breathing fast and clutching her bag, hoping and praying the rain wouldn't penetrate to her artwork.

"The door is open," Tom said as she ran past the outside bench.

She burst into the dark of the interior, swiping at the water on her face. "Oh my goodness." She set her bag to one side for fear of dripping on it and soaking the paper within. "I am wet through."

"It certainly was a deluge." He half laughed and placed his book and quill next to her bag on the table.

His shirt was clinging to his body, making it appear almost as if it had been painted on—sheer paint, almost opaque paint. His nipples were visible, hard little dots, as was the scribble of hair on his sternum. A drip ran from his brow, past his left eye and to his cheek. He dashed it away and studied her in the same manner she was studying him.

"Your...gown," he said then bit on his bottom lip.

Elizabeth looked down. "Oh my Lord." The wet material was clinging to her bosom the way his shirt was sticking to him. Luckily, it wasn't nearly as sheer, but still, her nipples poked at it. Small stiff points. Hurriedly, she crossed her arms over her chest.

"I should get you a towel," he said.

"Yes. Thank you. I would be most grateful."

But he made no move to get her a towel. He stepped closer. He was still breathing fast, and his wet cheeks were touched with redness.

She stared up at him, and a little thrill, one she hadn't felt before, went through her. It twisted in her chest and belly. He was gazing at her with such intensity. The kind of intensity she'd always dreamed of.

And he was so handsome, so masculine, so broad and strong. Everything she'd hoped to find in a man.

"Beth," he said, his voice low and husky.

"Yes." Her heart rate picked up.

"I have..." Daringly, he cupped her cheeks in both of his hands. His big palms were damp and hot.

There was no part of her that wanted to shake him off. Her heart rate picked up, and she rested her hands on his tendon-thick forearms. He was standing so close, it was quite improper, but oh, it was lovely to be so near to him.

"I have just produced some of my best work," he said quietly. "Sitting in the forest with you." His eyebrows drew together, his eyes narrowing slightly. "I feel like you have been sent to me, by God, to be my muse."

"Your muse?" Her voice was barely a whisper.

"Aye, my muse. My beautiful, delicate, captivating muse. You have no idea how many emotions you stir in me."

She swallowed and stared into his eyes. "And that's a good thing?"

"Aye, it's the best." He brought his face to hers, his lips hovering over her mouth. "The best thing for me and my poetry."

"Tom," she managed, her breath mingling with his. "I—"

"I want to kiss you," he said. "Say that I can."

"Kiss me...?" A strange heat filled her, longing gripped her. This was what she'd been waiting for. Tom was *who* she'd been waiting for. He was all wrong for her, but he was also so right.

"Beth?" he murmured. "Please." He screwed up his features, as though it would physically pain him if he didn't kiss her.

"Yes. Kiss me."

Very gently, he brushed his lips over hers.

She gripped him tighter and closed her eyes.

He held her face firmly, as though keeping her exactly where he wanted her, and probed his tongue into her mouth.

She moaned softly and opened up, let him in. The kiss deepened, and she pressed closer to him, her breasts squashing against his wet chest.

"Beth," he murmured, breaking the kiss for a moment before capturing her mouth again.

Desire shot into her system; it was thick and potent and brought with it a longing for more. Tom was everything she wanted. The feel of his solid body was intoxicating, and she ran her hands over his shoulders, down his back, learning the shape of him.

He did the same, and slid his hands down her neck so his thumbs rested on her collarbones.

"You're exquisite," he said, looking at where he touched her. "In every way, how you move, speak, smile, I could get drunk on watching you, being with you, writing poems about you."

"You could?" She was dizzy with joy. It seemed her attraction for Tom was reciprocated.

"Aye." Sliding one hand lower, he cupped her right breast over her gown. "I really could."

"Oh...Tom. I..."

"Tell me to stop if you need to."

"No...no, I..."

He smiled then kissed her again.

A moan escaped her throat. The way he was caressing her breast sent hot ribbons of pleasure to her belly, then lower, to between her legs. Catching in that place she longed to be touched.

She pressed her thighs together. She was heating up, dampening. Her nipples were hard pebbles, and he was fingering one of them through the material of her gown. So many times she'd wondered about a man's touch, but never had she thought it would be this good.

"I know we've only just met," he murmured and kissed across her cheek. "But this feels so right. You feel so right."

She tipped her head as he kissed the angle of her jaw, soft peppering touches of his lips.

His exploration of her body continued, one hand gliding to the first rise of her buttocks, and the other slipping under the neckline of her gown.

"Tom." A stuttered sigh left her mouth at the feel of his hand on her flesh.

He caught her nipple between his fingers, gently rubbing the pointed little twist of flesh.

"My beauty, my muse," he said, before once again kissing her.

She squeezed in close, caught up in the moment, wanting more, not wanting it to end.

But when she felt a solid wedge of flesh, hard and demanding and trapped between them, a rush of panic gripped her. She wasn't so naïve that she didn't know what it was he really wanted.

"Stop." She tore her lips from his and stepped back. The loss of his touch and body heat was almost a shock, even though it was her who had ended the embrace.

She blinked and looked around. Everything was the same as it had been when she'd stepped into the lodge. Long shadows, rain running from the roof, the dormant stove, a clutter of books and paper on the table.

"What is it?" he asked, holding out his hands to her.

"I don't know what came over me?" She put her hand over her mouth. "We really shouldn't have...you shouldn't have." She was breathing fast.

"Do not be remorseful." He frowned.

"How can I not be? We..." She swallowed.

"We kissed, that is all."

"But we...I am a..."

"You are what? A virgin?"

That wasn't what she was going to say, but he'd still hit a truth. "Yes."

"And you still are," he said. "One kiss does not stop you being a virgin."

"I should go home." She eyed the door over his left shoulder.

"It's still raining." His gaze dipped to her chest. "You can't go yet or like that."

"Darn it." Quickly, she pulled up the neckline of her gown, covering her bare right breast which poked rudely from her clothing. "It's passing. The storm. I really should go." She rushed to the door and yanked it open.

"No, please. You'll catch your death."

"I can't stay. I really can't."

She raced outside. With each step up the path, shame weighed heavier on her shoulders. How could she have got so swept away by a handsome gamekeeper? She was a lady, a young woman who had to marry well, and to do that she had to live a life free of scandal.

"Beth!"

If word of this got out...it would ruin her, and her parents. The Burghley name would be tarnished forever.

"Wait!" he called.

She dashed into the forest, splashing through muddy puddles. Another rumble of thunder, distant this time, sounded as though it was the first murmur of gossip about her.

Without looking back, she turned the corner and hurried along the wet track, tears spilling down her face and her body craving more of what Tom could give her.

# Chapter Six

Tom stood in the doorway, watching Beth leave. He could still taste her sweetness, his fingers were still warmed by her naked flesh, and his cock was hard and aching.

"Beth!" he called.

She ignored him.

"Wait!"

Should he chase after her through the rain? Make her explain herself? Why she'd suddenly become so skittish?

No. He had a feeling that would only worsen the situation. She was a startled deer, a timid wren.

He banged his shoulder onto the frame and rubbed his temple. She'd seemed to be enjoying herself. Hell, she *had* been. He'd felt the way she'd gripped him, kissed him. How her body had responded to his. A woman couldn't act that.

Yet almost instantly she'd retreated. Panicked. And now she was racing towards Littlemead.

But why?

They were adults. She'd encouraged him by turning up at his lodge so often, and the way she'd touched him, clung to him, these actions told him she'd wanted it as much as he had.

And it wasn't as though he'd spilled his seed inside her.

Feeling morose, he watched a goshawk dodge between the branches, silent and graceful as it sought a drier perch.

An empty hole grew in his stomach. Hollow. Pain. Confusion. He closed his eyes and saw her pretty face, heard her voice. His muse had left him.

"Exactly!" He slammed his fist into his palm. "And now I must write. I must get all of these emotions down on paper."

It might just be the makings of his next poem, this ghastly situation.

He raced inside, sat at the table, lit a candle, and began to write. He poured his emotions out, closing his eyes and capturing the gnarly, gnawing loss and the twist of confusion.

After a few minutes he poured wine. Sat again.

On and on he wrote. Pages and pages, stringing it all together until finally he'd finished. A poem he was proud of, and paired with the one he'd written about her earlier that day—when she'd been painting—he had two more for his new book. One about love and beauty and femininity, the second about desertion, hurt, and angst.

When he stood and stretched out his aching back, he spotted her bag. "Ah, so you will come back."

She'd have to. He knew his Beth well enough to know she wouldn't be parted from her paints for long, and even more than that, the new picture of lady's orchid was precious.

If he'd known where she lived, he'd have taken it himself. The rain had stopped now. But he didn't, so he'd wait until she knocked on his door.

* * * *

Elizabeth alighted her chaise with Sarah and stared up at the familiar church steeple. She'd barely slept a wink. Tossing and turning and her mind spinning with thoughts of Tom and what they'd done. She went from quivering at the memories of the way he'd touched her, the way he'd made her feel. To closing her eyes and groaning at her wanton behaviour.

She'd never been in such inner turmoil. If she had no other concerns, if she were the type of woman to throw caution to the wind, she'd have turned back halfway to home and let him do whatever he wanted with her.

She swallowed and closed her eyes. This was a place of worship, there was no way she could spend the morning thinking of the gamekeeper's mouth on hers and his oh-so wicked fingers toying with her breast.

"Lady Elizabeth, so good so see you."

She turned at the sound of a deep, familiar voice. "Baron Millbank, how well you look."

"Thank you, and so do you." He dipped his head in a small bow. "Summer has coloured your cheeks and your hair."

"It has been especially warm."

He glanced around. "Lady Elizabeth. Your parents are not here."

"No, they're in London, they had several engagements to attend."

"Ah, in that case, please allow me to escort you into church." He held out the crook of his elbow.

"Thank you, Gerald." She nodded at Sarah to hang back.

They stepped through the lynch gate and past a large old tomb covered in moss, the weathered writing on it barely legible.

"I understand you have a new gamekeeper," she said, wondering why in God's dear name she'd brought up Tom. It was as though he'd weaved his way into her mind and was spilling out of her mouth.

"Gamekeeper?"

"Yes, in Pheasant Lodge."

"He's a skilled hunter, naturally, being from the Highlands, but really, he isn't—"

"I met him when I was out painting, hunting for rare flowers." She decided to rush the subject on. "Quite tricky to find some of them. The animals eat the shoots, and then that's it for the year. But I've pretty much finished now. I do hope you don't mind me wandering onto your land with my paints."

"How could I possibly mind?" He smiled at her. "We have been friends since we were children."

"That is true. And thank you. I'm hoping to get published soon. A London press perhaps."

"I wish you good luck. Seems to be all the fashion getting published at the moment."

"It does?"

"Yes, my good friend, the Duke of Farrington, also wishes for that. But if you've been to Pheasant Lodge then—"

"Good day to you both." Reverend Smythe *smiled at* them. For a short man of slight build, he had a booming voice. He held a gold-embossed Bible. "I trust you are well."

"Yes, thank you, Reverend," Elizabeth said.

"Your parents are in London, I believe."

"Yes."

"I look forward to seeing them next week." He nodded at the Baron. "And how is your mother?"

"Faring better but still too sick for church, I'm afraid."

"Then I will call on her very soon." He nodded at the people behind them.

"I'm sorry about your mother," Elizabeth said as they found a pew. "What ails her if you don't mind me asking?"

"It is gout, the doctor said. Very painful." He sighed and shook his head. "I will pray for her relief."

"So shall I." She paused. "Oh, and before the service starts, I should warn you, Mother is intending a ball very soon."

"Yes, I have received an invitation. It is next weekend."

"You have received it already. Gosh, I have no idea how she will organise it so quickly. The idea only just came to her, and now she is in the ton."

"Your mother's skills are not to be underestimated. Remember that time she planned a croquet afternoon for your birthday and your entire lawn was set up with a band, drama plays, there were rowing boats on the lake, and several peacocks strutting around."

"Oh my, yes, I do remember. Will your mother be well enough to attend the ball?"

"I don't think so. But I may bring an acquaintance if that is agreeable."

"A young lady?" She raised her eyebrows at Gerald. He was an eligible bachelor, and her mother had suggested a union several times. But Elizabeth had pushed the idea away. She couldn't see him as anything other than a friend.

And she wanted a lover.

If only Tom had the title of Baron. Maybe then there would be a chance for them.

The service started with a hymn. Then there were prayers and readings, another hymn and another prayer.

With her head bowed, hands clasped on her lap, Elizabeth had a sudden realisation.

She'd left her bag with her paint and paintings at Pheasant Lodge.

A small gasp caught in her throat. How could she not have realised sooner?

Gerald twisted to face her, eyebrows drawn together.

She averted her gaze and looked at her lap again. How could she have forgotten something so precious to her? She was foolish beyond belief.

Tom had no idea where she lived. Indeed, he believed she lived in the village.

Perhaps she should ask Gerald to fetch it for her. But no. He would want to know what she'd been doing there. It was scandalous enough that she'd been spending time with a man without a chaperone, but to have got wet through with him, kissed him passionately, let him...

Her breasts tingled, and her nipples hardened. Right there in church while the reverend was asking God's forgiveness for their sins.

Surely she was the biggest sinner of all sitting in church that morning. Reckless. Immoral. Lustful. Rash. What would become of her?

"Amen," she said with meaning when the prayer came to an end and promising herself to keep her immodest thoughts and actions under control.

But would she be able to?

# Chapter Seven

"My lady, I cannot find your leather bag. The one with your paints." Sarah wound her hands together, her face a worried knot.

"Do not fret. I believe I have left it where I last painted." Elizabeth managed a tight smile as she placed her church bonnet on the dresser in her bedchamber. "I shall retrieve it first thing tomorrow morning."

"Would you like me to come with you? You have walked on your own so frequently of late."

"No, it's quite all right." She'd spoken quicker and firmer than she'd intended to and then instantly regretted it. Having Sarah join her would surely ensure there'd be no repeat of the shocking kissing incident.

*But what if Tom said something about the kiss?*

"Very well." Sarah retreated to the door. "Would you like to take tea in your room?"

"Yes, thank you. I am tired, perhaps I'll rest this afternoon."

"I think you should, you've been quite flushed since the storm yesterday."

"I have?"

Sarah touched her cheeks. "Yes, it did you no good getting so wet. Shall I have Cook make a bone broth?"

"I don't feel in the slightest bit unwell except for being tired, but yes, a broth would be welcome."

Sarah nodded then left the room.

"Tom! What have you done to me?" Elizabeth flopped on her bed and touched her cheeks. They did feel a little warm, but that was probably because she kept reliving the kiss.

A kiss that had heated her to volcanic proportions and made her blood flow like lava. Her head had spun with it. He'd put her under a spell. He had from the first moment she'd seen him, and if anything, it was getting more powerful.

49

She grabbed a pillow and plonked it over her face let out a cry of helplessness.

What was she going to do? Her heart beat faster just thinking of him. Her body yearned for his despite it being a totally depraved and shameful longing.

If only she could stop time. Magic all social stigma away. Create a bubble just for them. No interference. No scandal. Nothing in their way.

But that couldn't happen. She and Tom might as well live on different stars they were so far away from any chance of being together.

How she wished they could be. She would consider selling her soul for the chance to have a husband such as him.

Which, of course, could never happen.

So she'd go and collect her bag tomorrow and resist his trickery of seduction and try and move on with her life.

"My lady?"

"What?" She lifted the pillow from her face. Sarah was standing at the end of the bed with a tea tray. "Oh...I...thank you."

"Are you sure you're quite well?"

"Yes. Yes. I'm just...thinking about the ball we're throwing next Saturday. There is so little time to prepare."

"I believe your mother left detailed instructions to Cook and the footmen. An order is with the florist, and the string quartet has been arranged. I think all will be well, and besides, she will be returning in a few days." She set the tray down. "What do you think you will wear for the ball?"

Elizabeth sighed and sat up, her arms locked behind herself. "Another dress. Another ball. No doubt many young bachelors devoid of personality, too."

Sarah gave a sympathetic sigh. "You never know, someone might capture your attention and you his. Someone tall and handsome and with a glint in his eye."

"Sarah." Elizabeth laughed. "A glint in his eye?"

"Yes, exactly that, my lady." She grinned. "Someone with wit and an adventurous, curious side. One who will take risks, travel, be true to himself yet love you with all of his self. That is what you need."

"Do you think?"

"Indeed. For you are intelligent, ambitious, and energetic. A husband must be able to keep up with you and love you at the same time."

"Thank you for saying that." Elizabeth took the floral cup and saucer Sarah held out to her. "And if there is such a man, I hope God sends him my way."

"I have faith that He will. But..."

"But what?"

"You might not find him where you think you will."

"Whatever do you mean?" She took a sip of tea, even though she was very curious as to what Sarah meant.

"The good Lord works in mysterious ways. Life doesn't always go down the path you think it will." She paused. "My mother, God rest her soul, used to tell me to go down the path of happiness, it will always be the right one."

Elizabeth stared out of the window at the tree-spiked horizon. "Even if it makes other people unhappy?"

"We each have our own life to live and only one at that." She added more water to the teapot. "Do you need me for anything else?"

"No, thank you, that will be all for now."

Sarah left Elizabeth alone sipping her tea and nibbling a biscuit.

*We each have one life to live.*

It was true, but they were words bound by complexity. For no one could truly live without considering others and how their actions would impact on the lives of those they cared about.

Elizabeth finished her tea and set it aside. Feeling weary, she lay on her side and stared out of the window. Soon her eyes were drooping, and she let herself drift off to sleep.

Almost instantly, Tom was there, in her dreams. His face flashing from brooding to smiling and concentrating to questioning and then concern to passion—a fierce passion that lit his green eyes to flames. She felt him around her, his presence an embrace, his lips touching hers. Her body arched towards his hard one. Wanting him. Pleading for him. It was as if they couldn't live without each other.

Emotions were at war. Her longing a tight string that was being reined in despite its strength. Frustration clawed at her insides, a wild beast that scratched and snarled. Why couldn't she have what she wanted?

Suddenly, he was being dragged away by an invisible force. He reached for her, his face twisted as he called her name silently.

She thrashed to get to him. Fought her bindings. Battled the gripping hands holding her arms, her legs, her ankles.

He was fading, being swallowed up by a great black void. But she felt his craving for her, his battle to be with her.

And then she was falling, not towards him but backwards, into a great black void of her own. She screamed and flailed, her heart racing, seized by panic.

She awoke. Gasping. Blinded by the daylight. Disorientated.

"Heaven help me." She pressed her hand to her chest, trying to calm her galloping heart. It was almost as if he were still with her, or at least a part of him, a manifestation of him.

Was this what love felt like?

Had she hopelessly, ridiculously, rapidly fallen in love with Baron Millbank's gamekeeper?

Surely that was the most preposterous thing to have ever happened to her...no, make that to happen to anyone.

But when she closed her eyes again, his face was there. His voice filled her ears, his words echoed in her mind.

There was only one thing for it. She'd have to collect her bag tomorrow and put an end to this nonsense before her parents arrived home and became suspicious of her trips.

Yes. That's what she'd do. She'd bid him farewell...forever.

* * * *

Elizabeth paused at the lake. The jay was on the rocks again, with a partner this time, and both had what appeared to be a caterpillar in their beaks. They must have found a stash and were enjoying a meal together.

She sighed. If only she were a jay and could be with any other jay she wanted to be with and not one she was matched with by society.

Continuing her journey, she pulled her shawl a little tighter. The day was cooler than it had been, as if the storm had freshened the air.

A skein of geese went overhead, shouting to one another as they went, and she glanced at the tiny bit of sky above her but couldn't see them through the trees.

And then she heard a shot. A gunshot.

She spun around anxiously. If there was hunting afoot, she didn't want to be mistaken for a target. Her dress was dark blue and her shawl a dusty pale brown.

Another shot.

There was nothing to be seen, so she hurried on her way. The sooner she got to the lodge and retrieved her bag the better.

It came into view, and just as she was summoning her willpower to resist Tom if he attempted to kiss her again, he suddenly appeared.

Carrying two grouse carcasses, he had a gun thrown over his shoulder. His white shirt was once again half untucked, undone by several buttons, and the sleeves were rolled up.

The moment he saw her, he came to an abrupt halt.

Her breath hitched. He was so fine. How could she resist him? "I
needed to—" She gestured to the lodge and swallowed tightly. "Collect
my bag."

"Aye, you do." He hoisted the gun a little higher and strode to the
wire that already held two pheasants and two rabbits. "I didn't know
where you lived, otherwise I would have brought it to you. I know it's
precious."

"Thank you."

He set the gun to one side then dipped his hands in a barrel of water, washing them. When he pulled them out, he shook the drips from
them, and they caught like diamonds in a shard of sunlight. "You really
are quite careless with your possessions, Beth."

"It seems that way."

He gestured to the lodge. "Come in."

"I'm not sure if that's a good idea."

He bit on his bottom lip, kind of smiled, and surveyed her up and
down. "I'll only kiss you again if you ask me to."

"Tom, we shouldn't have, and I—"

He held up his hand. "We most certainly should have, and I'll show
you why."

"You will?"

He didn't answer, just strode into the lodge.

She couldn't help but admire his taut buttocks in his buckskin
breeches. They were tighter than was the fashion, but that suited him
well.

Despite her earlier decision not to go into his home, she was drawn
into the shadows. The moment she stepped inside it was like being in
another world.

Their world.

The smell of the fire and baking bread was a balm to her nerves, and
when he handed her a glass of wine and drew out a chair at the table,
she found herself sitting. "I heard shots, in the forest. Was it you?"

"Aye, I'm the only hunter around here today."

She nodded and took a sip of wine. Once again it was exceptionally good. "So why did we have to kiss?" She drank again, the word 'kiss' as sweet as the claret.

"Because of this!" He held up his notebook.

"I don't understand."

"When you left." He sat heavily and shoved his hand through his hair. A section to the right stayed aloft like two fingers pointing upwards. "I was bereft, hurt, saddened, and so many other feelings. I'd wanted you to stay more than anything. And so I sat and I wrote, and I poured out my heartache."

"Your heartache?" She studied his eager face, the glint in his eye, his passion for the situation he'd found himself in. Had she really had such an effect on him?

It seemed she had.

"My heart." He banged his chest. "Was beating for you. You were all I could think of. When you left, my arms ached for you. My eyes ached to see you. My ears to hear your voice, now listen..." He flipped open a page in his notebook and took a deep breath. "To this..."

The most beautiful poem she'd ever heard began to flow from him. It spoke of adoration, captivation, passion and loss, and tragedy and grief. While he read in his deep but softly accented tones, she barely breathed, and her eyes misted. It was as if his words were weaving a web around her, capturing her within it, holding her hostage, making her feel like the only woman in the world.

When he'd finished, he blew out a breath, sloshed wine into a glass, and knocked back a hearty slug. "So, what do you think?"

It was clear her answer was very important to him. She wiped at a tiny tear that had just escaped. "It was really very beautiful."

He closed his eyes for a few seconds as though satisfied with her response, then, "Anything else?"

"It came from your heart, your soul. It was more than words, Tom."

"Aye, Beth, it was so much more than words, it was the very essence of life."

She was quiet, waiting for him to go on.

"Love is the essence of life, and you...in the name of the Lord, I never expected it when I came to Pheasant Lodge, and God knows I sat around for weeks waiting for something to happen, but the moment you appeared from the trees you have filled me with something that feels so like love, I am sure it is."

"Love?" Was she hearing him correctly? Had he been feeling the same way she had?

"Aye, I have never felt it for a woman before, but you inspire me, you make me want to simultaneously hold you, write about you, tell the world how amazing you are and how happy you make me feel."

"Tom...why are you saying all of this?" Her armour was crumbling with each passing second. Like ice having boiling water tipped over it.

"Because it is the truth. There are too many people in this world who don't speak their truth, don't you agree?"

She took a gulp of wine. "I do."

"So what's your truth?" He leaned his elbows on the table and studied her with an intensity that heated her from the inside out.

"My truth?"

"Aye. What do you want, Beth? Tell me the truth."

"I want...I want to live my life for me, not for someone else. I want to find happiness and wealth, not wealth as in possessions but in relationships, achievements, charity."

"Exactly." He stood, the chair legs scraping on the floor. "And this is why I admire you so. Many women, many people, act only for material possessions or they act for others, but there has to be some part of you that fights and takes what *you* want. And what you want is so admirable, Beth, so agreeable you must surely do that no matter what it takes."

She looked up at him as he paced to the door and closed it. The outside sounds ceased instantly, and the room darkened. Her heart rate picked up, excitement singing through her veins. "What are you doing?"

"I want to kiss you again."

She swallowed, her lips almost tingling in anticipation. It was what she wanted, too. To hell with everything else. "So you can write another poem?"

He huffed. "No, because I feel like I won't be able to breathe if I don't kiss you." He clasped his hand around the base of his throat as though suffering a real physical reaction.

His passion, his need for her, was thrilling and also intense. "You...you said you wouldn't unless I asked you."

He stared at her, a muscle flexed in his jaw. "So ask me."

"What if I don't want to?" Her heart was pounding so hard she could hear her pulse thudding in her ears, a wild drum.

"Don't you?" His brow creased.

She didn't answer but stood. Should she leave or should she kiss him? She didn't know. Her head spun; his words had seduced her. Society and propriety had faded away again. No, more than faded, they'd ceased to exist.

*One life. Take the path of happiness.*

What if she could take that path, just for today, and have that happiness? Surely a moment with Tom was better than nothing at all with him.

"Beth?" His voice was low; he didn't move. His arms hung straight as pokers at his sides.

She set down her wine and removed her shawl, put it on the table beside her bag. There was a devil in her, she was sure of it, and he was prodding her with his little fork. But she didn't mind, she took that nudge towards what she wanted.

She slowly undid the front bow on her gown.

It opened a fraction, revealing her slight cleavage.

His gaze dipped. "Ask me." It came out as a growl. "Now."

"Kiss me."

Within a second she was in his arms and his mouth on hers. He was wild and fervent, his embrace tight and strong as he lifted her into the air.

She giggled and wrapped her arms around his shoulders.

"You're all I think of in daylight hours, and at night I dream of you," he said onto her lips.

"I am the same."

"You are?"

"Yes."

"You have just made me a very happy man." And as if to prove it, he kissed her again, his tongue dancing with hers. He lowered her feet to the floor. The kiss intensified, their teeth touched briefly. He slanted his head to kiss her deeper.

The next thing she knew he was backing her up, encouraging her to sit on one of the soft armchairs. He broke the kiss to pull off his shirt and toss it to one side. His broad chest was right before her, acres of smooth skin and hard muscle. The sight of it sent delicious tingles winging over her body, and her palms itched to touch him.

"What are you doing?" she asked breathlessly and setting her hands on his chest, over his tight little nipples.

"I'm going to thank you for taking the path to my lodge, for spending time here, for inspiring me." He lowered to his knees, so he was between her legs. "And show you how much I adore everything about you."

"You are? I...oh—" She hitched a breath.

He'd slipped his right hand beneath the hem of her dress and positioned it over her stockinged ankle. He slid up her left calf, over her knee and to her inner thigh.

"Shh, just feel," he said, lifting to kiss her again. "Let me give you erotic pleasure."

"Erotic pleasure?" She stared into his mesmerising eyes. "I'm not sure if..."

"You're not sure if you want it or if I can give it?" His breaths were warm and laced with wine.

"Neither, I..." His fingertips were at the juncture of her thighs, touching the patch of hair there. "I want it..." That couldn't be denied, and she had given up trying. "And I'm sure you can..."

"I can give you pleasure beyond your wildest dreams," he said. "Pleasure that will curl your toes and make you think of only me, nothing but me and how I can make you feel." He paused. "Do you want that?"

She swallowed; her belly was trembling, her toes already curled in her shoes.

"Beth?" He slipped a finger between her cunny lips.

"Oh. Yes. I...I...I want that." Her voice was tight and stuttering. They weren't words she should be uttering, but that little devil had taken control.

"I know." He dipped his head and kissed the hollow of her throat. "I can feel that you do." He found her entrance and drove one long finger into her.

She groaned and let her head fall back to the chair. All of her mother's stern warnings and sage advice evaporated. Right now, here, in the lodge, her body had taken over. Lust and desire were ruling her and satisfaction a demanding need.

"Ah, you're so sweet," he said, pulling her gown to one side so he could take her nipple into his mouth.

She groaned, slid her fingers into his thick hair, and tugged at the roots. His hot wet mouth had her arching her back. She wanted everything he could give, resisting was futile.

He suckled and drew her nipple to a desperately hard point at the same time as he filled her needy cunny with his finger, the heel of his hand catching on the swollen bud that throbbed with longing.

She felt wild and feminine, wanton and desired. It was heady and exciting, and she parted her legs wider.

He added another finger, stretching her, filling her, and rocked his hand in fast, firm movements.

"Oh, Tom," she gasped. "That feels so..."

"Good?" he asked.

"Yes." She was panting.

"Then you'll love this." Suddenly, he dropped down her body, to sit between her legs on his heels.

"What are you...oh...?"

With his free hand, he'd pushed at her gown, shoving it up her pale thighs to expose her cunny.

She drew in a breath. The sight of his big, hair-coated wrist against her slender legs, his hand so lewdly working her cunny, was shocking but thrilling, and a new wave of hunger gripped her.

"Wider," he said and pushed at her thighs. "Let me in."

She did as he'd asked, and he leaned forward, shifting the position of his hand so he could lick her most delicate place.

"Oh, sweet Jesus," she gasped when he used his tongue to draw fast circles over her bud. "Never have I thought...oh...Tom...this is surely a most terrible sin." A tremble went up her spine.

"A sin?" He looked up at her, his mouth a little shiny with moisture. "Sinfully good, right?"

"Right, yes, sinfully good, do it again." She clasped his hair and bucked her hips to meet his mouth. If this was the one real day of her life, she was done with holding back.

He chuckled. "You're a wild one, my Beth."

And then he set to work, building up the pressure in her pelvis. Stimulating her inside and out. His two fingers pumped into her, their way eased by her arousal, and he sucked and licked her cunny lips and bud. Almost teasing her, taking her to the point it was going to over-spill, then retreating.

"Oh...oh...please." She drew up her knees, clasping them to his solid torso, wanting to fall over that precipice of orgasmic pleasure.

He must have sensed the desperation in her voice because he upped the tempo and pressure. And this time when she reached the point of pure bliss, he stayed with her, pushing her, thrilling her, and as she teetered on the edge, she held her breath, waiting for the rush of bliss.

It came hard and fast, her cunny gripping his fingers and her spine curling, thrusting her forward. She cried out, unabashed, unashamed. It was the most alive she'd ever felt.

He kept his face buried and drew out the climax until she'd sagged back on the armchair, panting, perspiring, twitching with aftershocks.

"You have brought out a fiendish devil in me," he said, withdrawing his fingers and kissing her pubic hair.

"I have?"

"Aye, it's hardly proper to put your face between a lady's thighs, but I felt possessed with the need to do it. To feel and see and hear you take pleasure."

She wriggled and adjusted her gown, all of a sudden feeling exposed. "It certainly was...pleasurable."

# Chapter Eight

Tom gazed up at the beautiful red-cheeked woman sprawled on his armchair. She was still panting from the orgasm he'd just given her.

His cock was so hard it hurt, but he wasn't going to do anything about it. Not now, not today. That could wait until he made her his wife.

Aye, it would shock his sister when he took her home to his estate, and it would likely set tongues wagging. For he, a duke, was supposed to marry a title, good blood, royal blood even.

But that wasn't going to happen now he'd met Beth. Despite being a mere village girl, she was the one for him. She'd stolen his heart, become his muse, and he didn't want to live another second without her.

The only person he thought would be pleased for him was his friend, Gerald. He understood Tom's obsession with poetry and the long, lonely periods he'd endured.

"I feel like you've brought out the devil in me, too," she said and adjusted the neckline of her gown so her sweet bosom was covered. "I promised myself to collect my bag and nothing more."

"You did?" He raised his eyebrows.

"Yes. But it seems I can't trust myself around you."

"I like that." He grinned.

"You would." She laughed, though there was some tension in the sound.

He hoped regret wasn't seeping into her thoughts.

Standing, he reached for their wine and handed her glass to her. "Here, take a drink, relax. You can stay here the night."

"I really can't." She shook her head wildly.

"Why not?"

"People will wonder where I am."

"Where do they think you are now?" He sat opposite her, content to watch her mouth as she spoke and drank.

"My parents are out of town but returning tomorrow."

"Ah, I see. While the cat is away the mice will play."

"I suppose." She gestured around. "But I like being here. There's something about the simplicity that's comforting."

"Mmm." He glanced at the stove. He was more comforted when he had a cook, a butler, a maid, and footmen, but needs must if he wanted solitude and peace. "What is your home like, Beth?"

"It's also comfortable." She smiled, though there was sadness in the tilt of her lips. "I won't be able to visit tomorrow."

"The day after?"

"No, I have to help my mother, there are tasks to be performed."

He frowned. "Tasks?"

"Yes, of course." She sipped her wine. "There's always tasks."

"Like milking and sowing and weaving?"

She didn't answer.

*To hell with it. I'm just going to do it.*

"I think, Beth, that we should..." He put his wine down then slipped to the floor in front of her, one knee bent. He took her right hand in his, her fingers slim and delicate and her nails short and neat.

"What are you doing?" She set her shoulders back, her spine pencil straight.

"I think we should wed. It's obvious we're right for each other. A good match, and—"

"Wed! A good match? Are you crazed?"

It hadn't been the reaction he was expecting. "No, I am not crazed, nor deranged, nor of unsound mind, thank you very much."

"You must be." She yanked her hand away. "To even suggest marriage. We've only known each other a short time."

"Beth? Please." He ran his hand through his hair. Damn, it was messy, a bird's nest. No wonder she was hesitating. He must appear a fright. "I don't care how long we've known each other, but you should know I can give you so much. A fine house, good food, a safe place for children to grow."

"Strewth, you have us married with children already." She pushed to standing and stepped around him.

"Aye." He also stood. "Isn't that the natural way? One finds a life partner, marries, produces heirs."

"Life partner? Heirs?"

He closed his eyes and shook his head. Should he tell her of his title? Of his fortune? Surely that would win her over.

"I have to go." She swiped up her shawl and bag.

"Please, I beg you, don't rush off again."

"I shouldn't have come. We can't be together."

"I disagree. I disagree wholeheartedly."

"That is not my problem."

"Don't go," he said in a tone he hoped she'd obey. "If you do, I will come after you. I will ask your parents for your hand."

"Are you crazed?"

"You already asked me that, and I assured you I was not." He placed his hands on his hips and frowned. Frustration was mounting.

She clenched her fists and seemed as though she was stopping herself from stamping her feet. "I cannot marry you, and my parents would be in full agreement. For that I am deeply sorry, and it is something that will sadden me eternally, but it is a truth of the world we live in." She opened the door. "Out here we cannot be."

For a moment, the sight of her stole his breath. Highlighted by the sunshine, she was angelic with a halo around her golden hair and the tiny threads of her dress sparkling. He'd never seen anything or anyone more beautiful.

He'd never felt less able to make something his.

"Goodbye, Tom. I wish you every success with your poems."

"Forget the poems, I want you," he snapped. She had to know how much she meant to him.

"You can't have me." And with that, she was gone.

"Damn it." He rushed to the door.

She was already rushing to the path and within seconds had been stolen from him by the shadowy gloom of the canopy of trees surrounding the lodge.

He turned around and slammed the door. If he didn't, he would tear after her, hoist her over his shoulder, and bring her right back. Keep her with him, at his side for all of time.

But holding her captive wasn't a solution. He wanted to win her. Have her be with him of her own free will.

He swiped up his wine, drained it, then threw the glass across the room. It shattered against the wall, the last drip of claret running like blood down the white paintwork. For a second he felt marginally better for using up some of the hot energy galloping around inside him, but then he felt just as wretched.

"I'll write." He sat, hard, and reached for his quill.

Instantly words tumbled from him, filling up the page, random at first but then finding their way together and flowing smoothly. Each dip of his quill dampened some of his frustration and gave him something else to concentrate on.

He poured more wine and smelt her on his hand as he lifted the fresh glass to his lips. A new rush of inspiration came to him, his poem turning erotic and dark, a twist of love and lust and passion and desire. The ache of longing. The pain of separation. The wants and needs combined with forbidden fantasy and desperate craving.

When he'd finished, he pushed his work aside and stood.

Now was not the time to read it back or tweak it further. It had to settle, incubate, and when he was of clearer mind, he would perfect it.

"Perhaps I have yet another poem for my book." He reached his hands over his head, interlocked his fingers, and stretched with a groan.

What was he to do now?

He glanced around. Beth had said she liked the lodge, the comfortable simplicity of it, but right now the walls were closing in on him. Suddenly, he felt suffocated by it. The silence was deafening, and the small windows and dusky light oppressive.

Making a sudden decision, he scooped up his shirt and pulled it on.

Within minutes, he was striding in the opposite direction to the way Beth had gone. The track was narrow, and many woodland creatures had left footprints dotting the earth. He spotted another patch of lady's orchid on a slope beside a ribbon-like waterfall. The sight of it creased his brow, and he marched quicker, his strides long and purposeful, his jaw so tight he had to consciously release it for fear of breaking his teeth.

She'd refused his proposal. In an instant. She hadn't even given it thought.

That stung as if a whip had been slashed over his naked back. Never in his life had he even considered marriage, never been close to proposing, despite knowing many of the young ladies he met at balls would have agreed with only just a little stepping out together.

But Beth...he knew she was right for him, mind, body, and soul. What was worse was that he believed she knew it, too.

Eventually, The Millbank Estate came into view. He hoped to heck that Gerald was home. He needed company, and the company of a good friend at that.

As he approached, he tucked his shirt in and refastened the buttons. He rolled down the sleeves and buttoned the cuffs, but there was nothing he could do about the hopelessly creased material.

Stepping onto the gravel driveway, he spotted the groomsmen putting the horses out to pasture.

"Thomas, what are you doing here, old chap?"

Tom turned at the sound of Gerald's voice.

He stood in white breeches, navy coat, and waistcoat, and had a panting black gundog at his side.

"Ah, good, you are here." Tom wandered over to him and gave the dog a ruffle on the top of its head. He held out his hand to Gerald who shook it warmly.

"And so are you—here, that is. Which is a surprise. I thought you were staying at Pheasant Lodge until the end of the summer to write your book and that you wanted no interruptions, casual or otherwise."

Tom huffed.

"Ah, okay. The writer's block hasn't lifted, huh."

"Not at all, I mean it has lifted. The poems are pouring out of me."

"Then why are you so glum?" Gerald frowned.

"I...it's just...damn it."

Gerald clasped him on the shoulder. "Come on, let's drink port, and I'll see if I can help. I am a man of great wisdom and experience, you know." He laughed.

Tom didn't. "I very much doubt you can help, but a port sounds good."

They wandered around the south side of the enormous house, past great urns spilling over with summer flowers and glossy green ivy and seated stone lions perched on huge pillars—the seated lion was on the Millbank crest of arms and had been used excessively, or so Tom thought, around the house.

French doors were open to the library, and between them, a wrought-iron table and chairs. Tom took a seat while Gerald went inside to pour them a drink each.

When Gerald sat, he crossed his ankles, took a drink, and studied Tom. "You look as though you've battled fiend and foe to get here."

"Do I?" Tom set his drink on the table beside a copy of *The Morning Post* and had a futile attempt at flattening his hair. It had been messy anyway, but having Beth drag on it, clutch it, pull the roots almost from his scalp as he'd pushed her to climax, had really not helped its unkempt state. The memory caused a stirring in his groin, and he shifted on his seat.

"Yes, I get that you creative types live in your own world when you're creating, but really, you're a duke, it's a jolly good job only I am seeing you in this state."

"For that I apologise." Tom sighed.

"Please, there is no need. I am more concerned about what's going on in your head." Gerald paused. "You said the writer's block has lifted, which is good, right? Your plan to be secluded, away from distraction, has done the job."

"Aye, it has."

"And the reason you're not racing back to Edinburgh to provide your publisher with the finished manuscript is...?"

"It's not nearly close to being finished, but I have made an excellent start."

Gerald nodded slowly as if waiting for him to go on.

Damn it. His friend knew him too well. He would keep probing until he knew the cause of Tom's fractious state.

"So are you going to try me?" Gerald asked.

"What do you mean?"

"I said I would see if I could help."

"And you always do. You're a good friend, the best." Tom managed a half smile.

"Blazes!" Gerald sat forward and, holding his drink, pointed the rim at Tom. "It's a woman, isn't it? And don't deny it, only a woman can give a man like you such a forlorn expression." He paused. "Don't tell me she hasn't fallen for your charms."

Tom sighed heavily. There was no point denying it. "That's exactly what I'm telling you, only she has, did, I thought she felt the same, and then...oh, I don't know."

"Well, in the name of the Lord. You disappear into the forest for solitude and you come out in love. I would never have set my bets on that happening." He laughed as if it were a most excellent joke.

"Steady on, I don't know about love and—"

"Of course it is." Gerald's eyes sparkled, and he grinned. "So who is she? And how on earth did you meet her? Is she a seductive woodland pixie? A pretty little nymph?"

"I could have been fooled into thinking she was both of those the first time I saw her at the lake." Tom sat back and closed his eyes, reliving the memory of seeing Beth holding up her gown and paddling, the light on her delicate features making her resemble a china doll. How he'd longed to touch her from that first moment.

"What's her name?"

"Beth."

"And her family name?"

"I don't know." He shrugged. "She's from Littlemead."

Gerald scratched his chin. "I know most of the villagers but not a Beth. Perhaps she's visiting for the summer."

"Her parents live there, apparently."

Gerald looked thoughtful for a moment and then, "So you met her, fell in love, and what has happened to make you seek my company instead of hers?"

Tom swallowed. The next bit was like nettle rash to admit to. "I proposed. She said no."

"You did what?" Gerald slammed down his drink and jumped up. "Strewth, I've known you to be hot-headed and rash in the past, but you proposed, to a village girl you can't have known more than a few weeks."

Tom shrugged.

"And she said no. Why on earth would she say no to the Duke of Farrington, one of the wealthiest men in the Highlands of Scotland, master hunter and crafter of poetry read by gentry? I mean...why?"

"I think I know." He stared out at a copse of ancient oak trees. Several deer were grazing around them.

"Pray tell."

"I didn't tell her I was titled."

"You didn't?" Gerald sat with a bump.

"No, it didn't come up, and things were going so well, conversation flowed, she's intelligent and witty, talented, too, as well as being beautiful, so pretty my heart almost stopped beating when she smiled at me."

"Ah, you've got it bad. You need to get yourself to the village and tell her the truth. She'll marry you then, when she knows she'll never have to milk a goat or sow a field again."

"And is that really how I want to win a wife? Isn't that like buying a wife?"

Gerald was thoughtful. "Yes, you have a point, old chap. Which is why money marries money, there's no ulterior motive then."

"Which means I can't have her. Will never have her." He closed his eyes and rested his head back, letting the sun warm his cheeks. Would that be something he'd ever be able to live with?

He wasn't sure.

"And talking of money, Lord and Lady Burghley are throwing a ball on Saturday night. Why don't you join me as a guest?"

"No, I really don't think—"

"Don't say no just because you're mooning over a village girl. The company will do you good, and the wine will be top class. Lady Burghley has exquisite taste." He paused. "And their daughter is also a fine young woman, she might just take your mind off your heartbreak."

Tom wasn't sure if he wanted his mind taking off his heartbreak. He wanted to wallow in it a bit longer, use it to write, or better still, use it to figure out a way to win Beth back.

"It will do you good to be seen with the right people while you are visiting this neck of the woods, even if at just one social occasion in the round of balls."

"That is true."

"So it is settled, though I must insist a visit to the barbers, Tom, otherwise they might not let you through the front door."

# Chapter Nine

"My goodness, what an exceptional estate," Tom said as the chaise was trotted up the sycamore-lined driveway to Burghley House.

In old Gothic style, it rose majestically from the surrounding green landscape. The ornate house, that held many ornaments, was made from large cream stones common to the region, and the main entrance was set back, as though the house was in the shape of an H with the door being on the narrow middle bar.

Except there was nothing narrow about it. Tom's Highland home was vast and sprawling but this one even more so. It was at least two storeys higher and had many more chimney pots. The windows were large, and the walls leading off to the sides suggested impressive kitchen gardens.

"It is indeed," Gerald agreed. "It has been in the Burghley family for many generations."

"And they make their money from land, you said."

"Yes, they own many hundreds of acres, in fact, south of Littlemead, the village your love is from, they own to the border of the county. It's leased, and there are many tenant farmers, and I believe Lord Burghley also has some profit-shares these days."

"I think it is obvious she is not my love." Tom's mood—which had lifted as he'd prepared for a night away from the lodge—dived again. Beth had kept her word and hadn't been back to see him. Gerald had offered him one of the many guest rooms at The Millbank Estate, but he'd declined as he wanted to be at the lodge if she emerged from the shadows of the trees as she was fond of doing.

He could only pray that sense would come to her and she'd see they were meant for each other.

And then he would tell her she'd be a duchess once they were wed. Oh, he could hardly wait to see her face.

The chaise came to a halt, and a footman opened the door.

71

Gerald stepped out, so did Tom. The sun was kissing the horizon and the shadows long and tinged with pink and lilac.

"I will soon ensure you are acquainted with all the principle people in the room," Gerald said, striding forward and looking dapper in his eveningwear.

Tom followed, his kilt, a tartan of forest green, navy, black, and pale yellow, swished as he went. He wasn't expecting to know anyone at the private ball as his usual haunts were Edinburgh or London. But still, he agreed with Gerald, a dance and lavish supper would do him good.

They entered the grand hallway lined with fine art and were offered champagne, which they each took. Already a string quartet was playing; the first dance would soon be underway.

"Remember you are an eligible bachelor, my friend, take your pick."

"I have no interest in marriage at present, and you know why."

Gerald scowled at him. "That state of mind is best kept to yourself at a ball. This is basically a marriage market, and you are a fellow in possession of a good fortune to purchase what takes your fancy."

"As are you, my friend. Are you buying at this market?"

Gerald nodded a greeting at a gentleman to his right. "I have yet to find the duck to my fox."

Tom chuckled. "I hope you find your duck one day."

"So do I, old chap."

The ballroom was substantial with a lofty muralled ceiling, gold-leafed embellishments surrounded portraits on the walls, and five dazzling chandeliers shone like stars. Gold-threaded drapes hung at the massively high windows, and on the right a huge fireplace, large enough to stable a horse, was dripping with flowers. Opposite this, glass doors had been flung open to a balcony overlooking a lake.

A crowd of people, a hundred he'd guess, and at least half of which were ladies in a rainbow of coloured gowns, lined the edge of the room, chattering gaily and sipping champagne.

"There's the hostess," Gerald said. "The Duchess of Burghley."

A slight woman with pretty ash-blonde hair stepped into the centre of the dance floor. Her dress reminded Tom of a bumble bee; it was bright yellow with a vertical black stripe from floor to bosom, and the sleeves had black and yellow ribbons hanging from them. Like all the women she wore gloves; hers were black.

"My esteemed acquaintances," the master of ceremonies said loudly.

The room quieted

The hostess smiled. "I would like to offer my deep gratitude for your attendance. Certainly, I gave you sinfully short notice, but the weather was just too fine to miss the opportunity to dance all night, and unlike the ton, we do not get as many chances for a ball." She beamed and seemed to study each face in turn in only a few seconds.

Tom felt her gaze pass over him, pausing for the tiniest of moments.

"So my husband, Lord Burghley, myself, and my daughter would like to wish you all a very enjoyable evening. Please, let's start." She signalled to the band.

The music rang out. Couples who had already agreed to dance together stepped forward, arms linked, and then set up a line facing one another.

Tom glanced to his right. Two young women stood alone, hems hooked and dance cards hanging from wrists. An older woman stood with them, their mother perhaps. He held in a sigh. They were young, likely their first season, but it was dutiful to dance.

Gerald had seen them, too, so the two men stepped up, and each gave a small bow.

"Mrs Brentwood, a pleasure to see you," Gerald said.

"And you, Baron Millbank." She smiled and turned her attention to Tom.

"This is the Duke of Farrington, Thomas Kilead."

She inclined her head again. "It is a great pleasure, your grace."

"The pleasure is all mine." Tom smiled.

"These are my daughters, Eloise and Charlotte."

Gerald politely greeted the two girls then held out the crook of his elbow to Eloise.

She beamed and slipped her hand through it.

"Would you care for this first dance, Charlotte?" Tom asked.

She looked at her mother who nodded, almost imperceptibly, but it was there. "Why thank you," she said and took his arm.

The dance began with Tom and Charlotte and Gerald and Eloise at the farthest end of the room, near the entrance.

But the dance was a twist on the cotillion and involved weaving and wending along. Soon Tom and Charlotte had moved several couples in.

The graceful steps and the wonderfully performed music were a far cry from the way Tom had been living of late. Part of him was happy to settle into what he knew, the other part of him longed for Pheasant Lodge. For his comfortable worn clothes, the sound of the birds, and his squishy fading armchair.

An armchair he'd sat his love upon before tasting her, caressing her, feeling her pleasure.

Heat travelled up his back, around his neck and to his cheeks. How he missed her. If he'd never kissed her or touched her, would the ache still be as painful?

Charlotte cleared her throat.

Damn it, he was supposed to be engaging in conversation, not thinking about burying his face between a village girl's thighs.

"The weather is pleasant," he managed.

She gave him a look, only briefly, that reminded him weather talk was boring.

"And this room, it's so stylish," he added and spotted Gerald raise his eyebrows at him.

"Yes," Charlotte said, stepping around him and then rejoining the line of ladies opposite.

They moved forward, held hands, spun around, and took three steps. "You and your sister are very similar."

"Yes, we are twins."

"I see. And what age are you?"

"We turned eighteen last month."

It occurred to him he had no idea what age Beth was. She was older than Charlotte, he was sure. Whereas Charlotte and her twin sister still held a girlish softness to them, Beth was a woman. That didn't detract from her beauty, indeed it added to it. He guessed he was maybe a little older than her, but not by many years.

"Do you prefer not to converse while dancing?" Charlotte asked.

"Forgive me," he said. "I have had a somewhat distracting day."

"Oh?"

"Aye." He paused, and as he thought of an explanation, he glanced down the long row of dancers.

His heart skipped a beat then seemed to do another to catch-up. He stopped moving, utterly, and had to be prodded to take the next step. "My apologies," he managed.

It was hard to believe what he was seeing, but in the middle of the dancers, spinning graceful steps, was Beth.

Except it wasn't Beth, it couldn't be. It must be *her* twin. But a twin at a private ball hosted by Lord and Lady Burghley. How could that be?

"And your distraction was caused by...?" Charlotte asked.

"My what?"

"You said you'd had a distracting day?"

"Ah, aye, I have." He frowned and swallowed. Beth, if indeed it was her, appeared angelic in a pure-white gown and with tiny white flowers in her hair. He'd never seen anyone more breathtaking. She was smiling as she spoke to the man she was dancing with.

A sudden itch went up Tom's spine. Who was that man? He was taking her gloved hands, conversing as though they knew each other well, turning her gently each time the dance moved on.

He glanced at Charlotte when they came face to face then side-stepped. Her mouth was a tight slash, downturned at the corners.

"Forgive me," he said. "Tell me, have you travelled far to be here?" They came back in line and he once again glanced at Beth.

"Too far to dance with a man who doesn't want to dance with me," Charlotte said when they came close again.

"I beg your pardon?" He raised his eyebrows at her.

"Toddington. It's just a little way past the River Lyme." She smiled as though butter wouldn't melt.

"Oh, I see. Very nice."

Gerald gave him a questioning frown.

Truth was, Tom couldn't wait for the damn dance to end. He wanted an introduction to the woman in white, who unless his brain had been addled, was his Beth—the object of all his affections and desires and the woman he wanted to marry.

Finally, the music stopped and the dance drew to its conclusion. He bowed at Charlotte and made no move to fill in her dance card. She appeared as relieved as he was and turned to retake her spot beside her mother.

Impatiently, he waited while Gerald made polite talk with Eloise before escorting her back to her mother. The moment he turned away, Tom rushed up to him. "I need you to make me an introduction."

"You do?" Gerald's eyebrows rose. "Who?"

"Over there." He nodded towards the fireplace. Beth stood beside a cascade of pink and cream flowers talking with Lady Burghley, the hostess. "Her. The young lady in white. Do you now her?"

"Of course, I know Lady Elizabeth Burghley well."

"Elizabeth." He frowned. Elizabeth. Beth. Was it one and the same?

"Yes, she's Lord and Lady Burghley's only daughter. A year younger than I. We've known each other since childhood."

Tom stopped staring at Beth and instead stared at his friend. "And you never thought to introduce me to her previously?"

"How could I? You rarely visit The Millbank Estate. Usually we meet in Edinburgh or London or I make that insufferable journey to Kilead."

Tom placed his hand on his brow. "More fool me."

"You seem quite vexed."

"I am." He gripped Gerald's arm. "I need you to introduce me now, before the next dance. I need you to introduce me to Lady Elizabeth Burghley before I believe myself quite mad."

# Chapter Ten

"Viscount Delany is looking rather dashing tonight, don't you think, dear?"

"Mother," Elizabeth said, "he is so much older than I, plus I believe his heart is set on Miss Margaret Townsend."

"How could you know this?"

"He speaks of her every time we meet." Elizabeth smiled. "I only hope his affections are returned. I'm fond of him, he's a good man." Taking an offered glass of wine from a silver tray, she glanced around.

Walking towards her was Baron Millbank, no doubt coming to fill in her dance card, which was most agreeable. She could perhaps ask about his gamekeeper, if she worded it subtly, of course.

Next to him walked a man she didn't recognise. Tall and broad, dark hair cut neat, clean-shaven, and a beautiful golden cravat and waistcoat that complemented his kilt—except she did recognise him.

"Oh dear Lord." She swallowed and held her glass halfway to her mouth.

What on earth was Gerald's gamekeeper doing at a private ball?

Her mother's private ball.

He came closer. His attention set steely upon her and his lips a tight, straight line.

The two men came to a halt before Elizabeth and her mother. Seeming to loom above them.

"Elizabeth, my dear." Her mother touched her wine glass. "You are about to spill that."

"I...er...sorry." She righted the wine and gripped the stem. It wasn't just the wine that was threatening to land on the floor. Her knees had gone weak, as if they'd turned to slush.

Still *he* stared at her.

"Lady Burghley," Gerald said, bowing slightly at Elizabeth's mother. "Thank you once again for the kind invitation."

"It is my pleasure." She turned her attention to Tom. "And who, may I ask, have you brought as your guest?"

*Is it Tom?*

Out of context, away from the forest, Elizabeth doubted herself momentarily. But yes. It most definitely was Tom.

Her Tom.

Tom was Gerald's guest.

Her heart thudded, and her stomach clenched. What was happening? The room swayed slightly. Life was playing some kind of strange trick on her. A delusional fantasy had her in its steely grip.

"Lady Burghley, Lady Elizabeth, may I introduce the Duke of Farrington, Thomas Kilead."

"Duke?" Elizabeth croaked.

"Lady Elizabeth." Tom dipped his head but kept his eye contact steady with hers. "My absolute pleasure, and what a pretty name. Elizabeth."

"My name." She gulped. "I...thank you." She glanced at her mother who had a glint of curiosity in her eyes.

"And you're the Duke of Farrington," Elizabeth managed. "Did I hear that right?" She had to ask.

He straightened, cocked his head to the right. "Indeed you heard right. It seems we are both from the same world after all."

"After all? Why, have you...?" Gerald looked between them, "made an acquaintance in the past?"

"No!" Elizabeth snapped. Terror formed a ball in her stomach. What if Tom mentioned what they'd done? How wanton her behaviour had been. The scandal would be unbearable. Not for him, most likely, but she'd be ruined. So would her family name.

Tom pulled in a deep breath, his jacket expanding, and placed his hand on his hips. "No. I haven't had the pleasure until now."

She nearly sighed with relief. The emotion was brief, though, because one glance at Gerald and she could see the cogs of his mind working. He was putting together her mention at church of the gamekeeper at Pheasant Lodge. The man was no fool and had a good memory to boot.

Darn it.

He clearly had known his friend was staying there. Writing poetry. And he wasn't a gamekeeper at all. He was a duke, a man of wealth and standing and no doubt had gamekeepers of his own.

Oh, in the name of the Lord, was it too late? Had Tom spilled the beans to Gerald already? Told him what they'd done? Was it too late to salvage her reputation?

"Do you remember at church, Elizabeth, that I told you my friend considered getting published to be quite the fashion?" Gerald asked. "This is he."

"I see." Her mouth was dry. She gulped a mouthful of wine and nearly choked on it. "How...how interesting."

"But you must know that as you said—"

"May I?" Tom interrupted, gesturing to her dance card.

"I..." She shook her head, a frown ploughing over her brow. She felt sick, goose bumped, as if her body wasn't her own. "I don't know, I..."

"Elizabeth, dear, the Duke of Farrington would like a dance." Her mother nudged her. "I think it would be an excellent idea."

"You do?"

Her mother studied her inquisitively. "Yes. Give him your dance card, my dear."

Elizabeth did as instructed.

Tom filled it in, so did Gerald.

Taking it back, she read the list.

Her dance with Tom was the very next one. However would she manage to be so near to him? He was all she thought about day and night. Her heart had broken in two when she'd walked away from the man she loved and who loved her but she could never be with.

"Baron Millbank," her mother said. "Can I introduce you to Carrie Newton and her mother? They have travelled from Staffordshire to be here. Terence Newton made his money in cotton, I'm sure you'd be quite interested to hear about it."

"Yes. Thank you. I'd like that very much." Gerald offered his arm to Elizabeth's mother and then nodded to Elizabeth as they excused themselves.

She tipped her chin and looked up at Tom. "What are you doing here?"

"The same as you." The tendon flexed in his cheek, the one that jumped when he was frustrated or mad or concentrating. "Dancing, drinking, making new acquaintances, or in our case, reacquainting."

"Why didn't you tell me you're a duke?" She'd spoken through gritted teeth then quickly tried to get her mouth to relax should anyone be watching their interaction.

"And why didn't you tell me you were a lady from a family of great wealth?"

"You didn't ask."

"Did you ask?" His calm tone was maddening.

"Yes. I believe I did."

"Then it slips my memory."

She took a step closer. "You led me to believe you were a gamekeeper, an employee of Baron Millbank."

"You supposed that because I was staying in a gamekeeper's lodge. I never said he was my employer."

"So why were you there?"

"You know full well."

"I do?"

"Aye, to write. As it turned out, everything I wrote, every single word was about you."

"Lords, ladies, and gentlemen, take your places for the next dance, please."

"I don't want to dance with you," she said, finishing her wine and pursing her lips.

"I think you would like to cause a scene less."

She glanced at her mother who was smiling at her.

"One dance," she said. "Then you must leave."

"Is that what you really want?"

"Yes." She didn't take his arm as she found a spot on the floor between two ladies facing the row of men.

He stepped past her, his arm brushing hers, and took his position directly opposite her.

"Now for the allemande," the master of ceremonies called. "Would the first couple please lead off."

The music started, and the dance began with the first couple walking and turning and sidestepping down the centre. Other couples followed suit in an elaborate twirl of straight-backed bodies, all with chins held high.

When it was their turn, Tom held out his hand.

She had no choice but to take it.

"You look beautiful in a ball gown," he said when his face came close.

"We do not have to talk during this dance." She spun away, stepped twice, then turned to face him again.

They waited a moment as another couple took their turn.

When they came close again, he said, "You're right. We should probably talk in private, later."

"I do not think so." She had to stop herself from frowning.

"I thought I was never going to see you again."

"That would have been for the best."

The dance required him to take several steps back. Hurt crossed his face, his lips pressing together and his eyes narrowing.

Her heart squeezed. The last thing she'd wanted to do was hurt Tom. And she truly believed she had, almost as much as it had hurt her to turn down his proposal and leave him.

But now...now that hurt inside her had expanded until it touched every surface of her organs. He'd lied. How could he have been so deceitful?

And to turn up at her mother's ball. At her home and shock her like this. That was unforgivable. All he'd had to do was ask Gerald to pay a visit and he could have come and spoken to her in private. Because this torture of dancing with him, in front of her parents, in front of everyone she knew when only a few days before he'd had his face, his fingers...his tongue...

She closed her eyes and stiffened her resolve. It was a long dance, true, but she'd see it to the end.

"You look like you want to walk away," he said. He took her hands again.

"How can I?"

"You have legs." He glanced downwards.

Oh, he was maddening. "And cause a scene, I don't think so. That would bring even more attention to us. Not that there is an us."

"I would heartily disagree."

"I expected you would."

"My lovely Beth, I asked you to marry me, that certainly means there's an us."

"Please keep your voice down," she practically hissed.

"Why?"

"Because if my mother hears you say that—"

"She will be overjoyed, no doubt. A duke for a son-in-law, surely that is good enough for Lady Elizabeth Burghley."

"What she doesn't know is you're a liar, and a sneaky, contriving one at that."

His mouth opened, but no words came out. He closed it again.

She turned away, took several paces around other dancers, weaving this way and that, then came back to him.

"I do not know why you should think that of me." His voice was strained.

"You're here, aren't you, trying to embarrass me at my mother's ball."

"I am doing no such thing."

She stepped back. They'd returned to their original places in the line, and the music stopped, signalling the end of the dance.

Around her the hum of conversation rose. Couples linked arms and moved off in search of refreshments.

She wanted to turn away but found herself staring up at him.

After a moment he stepped close. He didn't take her hand. Instead, he leaned to speak into her ear.

She pulled in a breath. His cologne was the same as it always was, rich and spicy, and it made her heart flutter. She closed her eyes and held her breath.

"If I wanted to embarrass you," he whispered, "I'd have made mention of the fact that only a few days ago I had my face between your legs and you were dragging on my hair and crying out my name in ecstasy. That is the subject I would bring up to truly make your cheeks red."

She gasped, her hand coming to her chest. "You wouldn't dare."

His eyes flashed, something between amusement, devilishness, and desire.

Grabbing a glass of wine from a passing waiter, she stepped away. She was hot and flustered, her gown too tight and heavy, and her scalp itching where pins held her hair in place.

With her hem held slightly aloft, she scooted past neigbours and friends and cousins. She needed air, cool fresh air.

The darkness of the night beckoned her, and she stepped out onto the balcony, then walked to the far end, away from the lights of the interior. She had a sense of her world falling apart. A hammer had come down on it, sending fragments scooting in every direction.

The balcony had been as lavishly decorated as the ballroom, summer blooms and ivy winding around the old stone rail and the urns overflowing with flowers. Several flickering candles were sheltered by storm lanterns and placed in corners. Moths fluttered around them.

Her breaths were coming fast and uncomfortable as she rushed on. Tom's words rattled around her brain. How could he have uttered them in the ballroom? What if someone had overheard his wicked description of her antics? Then where would she be?

The stone rail was cold, and she gripped it over the flowers and slugged on her wine. It was only a mouthful, but she needed it. "Dear Lord," she murmured, staring up at the stars—bright pinpricks in a black velvet cloth. "Please help me."

"Beth."

She turned and saw a large frame stepping out from the brightness of the ballroom. "Leave me alone, Tom." She glanced around, hoping no one could hear her address him so casually.

They couldn't. They were the only people outside. Everyone else was enjoying the spread of food before the next dance.

"If memory serves me right," Tom said, "this is the third time you have run from me. It's becoming a habit." He walked across the balcony into the darkness and came to a halt before her. "And for the record, I don't like it one bit."

"I don't care what you like, you need to leave. How could you show up here and say such things? Have you no morals?"

"Shall I add lack of morals to being a sneaky, contriving liar?"

"It seems fitting."

He stepped next to her and stared out at the night, gripping the balcony the way she had been. "Why are you behaving like this?"

"Because you've destroyed my world?"

"What? Because I want to marry you? Because you've stolen my heart?" He lifted his face to the sky and closed his eyes. "I haven't been able to stop thinking about you, but what could I do? I didn't think I'd ever see you again."

"You could have asked Gerald for an introduction to the Burghley family and done it in private."

"How could I?" He shook his head. "I had no idea you were Lady Elizabeth Burghley."

"I don't believe you. If Gerald is such a good friend, if you'd mentioned me then he would have—"

"I did mention you, but you told me your name was Beth, and I had no idea of your family name."

"Actually, I did no such thing. I told you my name was Elizabeth, you misheard, likely distracted with your poems, and besides, my father calls me Beth, so it's not totally wrong."

He dropped his elbows to the balcony and hunched forward as though needing the support. "Can we stop this? I want to be with you. I wanted to be with you when were were just Tom and Beth, in the forest, the rest of the world a distant memory."

"But that wasn't real, and this is."

"The fantasy can become reality."

"No. You lied, I can't get over that."

"But didn't you, too? I can get over it, please, Beth, let's—"

"Don't call me that. And you should leave." She tilted her chin. "And if you don't, then I will."

"It's your ball. You can't just leave."

"It's my mother's, and I'll say I feel unwell."

He paused for a moment then, "Please yourself, I'm not going anywhere. I'm in the mood for drinking, feasting, and dancing."

She scowled at him. Had she ever met anyone more stubborn? More annoying? "Then I'll bid you goodnight. Please apologise to Gerald that I won't be able to honour my dance with him."

With her shoulders back and chin held high, she stalked into the ballroom. A quick conversation with her mother pleading a headache, and she'd be able to remove herself from the nightmare she was living.

# Chapter Eleven

Tom woke after noon the next day with a thumping head. He'd drunk too much wine and danced until the sun was lighting the eastern horizon. He'd kept glancing at the entrance to the ballroom, hoping Beth might reappear.

She hadn't.

And she'd had the cheek to call him stubborn?

And a liar? Couldn't she see they'd both hidden something from each other? Didn't that make them equally in the wrong? And was it even wrong? They'd each confessed their desire for more than material wealth in their lives, so why should it matter to their relationship if they were both from rich families?

He sat with a groan and spotted a tray of tea on the bedside table. Hopefully it had been set down recently.

He poured. It was lukewarm. It would do, so he settled back on the pillow to drink it.

There was a knock at the door. Presuming it to be a servant, he called, "Come in."

Gerald stepped in looking far too bright for a man who'd danced all night. "Good morn to you, old chap."

"You're very sprightly." Tom frowned and drained his tea.

"And you definitely aren't." He walked to the window and shoved the heavy drapes half open.

Tom narrowed his eyes at the bright light. "Is that necessary?"

"So now that we are out of earshot of prying folk," Gerald said, turning with hands on hips, "are you going to tell me what in the devil's name is going on between you and Lady Elizabeth Burghley?"

Tom sighed.

"Strewth, is it that bad?"

"What do you mean?"

"You have the lovesickness that bad."

"Huh, does it look like she loves me?"

Gerald tapped his chin as if thinking. "Er, no, it really doesn't, she did seem rather shocked, surprised, and angry to see you." He dragged a chair over and sat. "I take it she's the Beth you mentioned. The one you met while at Pheasant Lodge." He paused. "Though I've only ever heard her father call her that name."

"Apparently so."

Gerald tipped his head. "She told you she was a village girl?"

"Not exactly, I just presumed."

"Ah!" He stood, paced to the right and then the left. He stopped and held up his right index finger. "It's all making perfect sense to me now."

"I'm glad it is to someone." Tom poured more tea. He needed the fluid.

"Yes. When Lady Elizabeth and I spoke at church, she made some comment about me having a new gamekeeper. Naturally, I didn't know what she was talking about. Now it makes sense, she was talking about you." He sat heavily. "Why in the name of Jesus didn't you tell her you're the Duke of Farrington? Why let her think you were a gamekeeper?"

"The subject didn't come up."

"The same way her being the only daughter and heiress to the Burghley fortune didn't come up?" Gerald raised his eyebrows.

Tom didn't even bother to answer and drank his tea in several big gulps.

Suddenly, Gerald leapt up again. Right into the air. He didn't stop when he landed, he did it again and then practically bounced around the bed. "Jesus, Mary and Joseph, I've just remembered."

"Will you stop blaspheming, you'll be struck down."

"I'm sure He will understand my shock." Gerald held out his hands and stared at Tom.

"What?"

"You proposed! That's what you told me when we were drinking port. You, the Duke of Farrington, asked Lady Elizabeth Burghley to marry you."

"And she said no if you remember."

"Yes, but don't you see?"

"See what?"

"She said no because she thought you a gamekeeper and there was no way her parents would allow such a union. But it isn't true, you are from a fine ancestry line, royal blood even, and you are a man of means, she will never have to worry about finances. You are an utterly perfect match."

"While I am enjoying the flattery, I am well aware of the situation, and can I point out she wasn't exactly rushing to accept my proposal yesterday evening when she found out my real status."

"Mmm." Gerald twisted his mouth and scratched his temple. "I see your point."

"Exactly. And if you recall, you missed your dance with her because she feigned sickness, preferring to leave the ball, her own mother's ball, than stay in the same room as I."

"Yes, more's the pity, I always enjoy a dance with Lady Elizabeth, and a good conversation, too. She's quite witty, up to date on *The Morning Post*, and what I like most is she doesn't take fools gladly. She is what my father would call high spirited."

Tom frowned. It irked him that Gerald knew her so well. "So why haven't you ever proposed if she's so fine and witty?"

"Oh, I might have got around to it one day, but we're friends, childhood friends. There's affection there, certainly, but not romantic affection. Perhaps if we both reach thirty and are still single we'll make a match." He grinned. "Yes, that would be very agreeable, she's certainly delectable."

"No you damn well won't." Tom threw back the covers and stood, headache forgotten. "I'm going to make her my wife if it's the last thing I do. No one else will have her."

Gerald clapped. "Yes, that's the attitude." He paused. "And how are you going to do that?"

"I'm going to go to the Burghley Estate now."

"Now?"

"Aye. I'll take a horse."

"And what will you do on arrival there?" Gerald sat and crossed his legs. The way he cocked his head and tapped his fingers on the arms of the chair suggested he was thoroughly enjoying the drama.

"I will...I will...insist that she takes my proposal seriously."

"And how will you do that?"

Tom frowned and strode to the window. The sun was high. A few long, straight clouds, like sweeps of white paint, hung over the trees. "I will reassert it for a start and hope that she sees it is for the best."

"For the best. I see."

"What do you see?" Tom turned.

"I just think it's going to take more than your assertion. She really does seem very vexed with you."

"And I don't know why. It's unjustified."

"The workings of a lady's mind are not always easy for us menfolk to understand, they're quite different creatures to us. So what I'd suggest is..." He paused.

"Go on."

"That you make it so she can't say no to your proposal."

"And how do you suggest I do that?"

"Take her to Kilead."

Tom laughed, but it was a hard, tight sound. "Just like that? Take her to the Highlands?"

"Yes." Gerald stood and gripped Tom's shoulders. "You need time with her. Time away from everyone else. You need to recreate Pheasant

Lodge. From what I gather, you had a rather lovely time talking about poetry and painting."

"Aye. We did." Tom frowned. It really hadn't been proper for them to spend so much time alone. And the last thing he was going to do was utter a word about what they'd really done to Gerald. That was between he and Beth.

"Take her to Scotland. You're a clever man, Tom, I'm sure you'll think of a way to get her there. And when you do, you can make her fall in love with you all over again."

Tom nodded. It wasn't a great plan, but it wasn't bad either. And Gerald was right, he needed to get her to fall in love with him again.

* * * *

Elizabeth sipped the herbal tea her mother was insisting she sup all day to cure her make-believe ails. It tasted of the earth and grass and made her stomach growl.

But it was better than having to have spent the night watching Tom dance with debutantes and her cousins and wonder if at any moment he might blurt something out about their time together—and in doing so create a vast hole that would suck her in, never to be seen again.

"Are you going to get dressed today, my lady?" Sarah asked.

"Yes, I should. Perhaps the dress from last summer, with the rose embroidery on the panel. It is really quite comfortable."

"Very good."

Sarah retrieved the dress and then helped Elizabeth into it. She then twisted her hair up on top of her head and held it in place with a silver clasp that had belonged to her grandmother.

"Thank you, that will be all." Elizabeth smiled.

"Shall I send tea?" Sarah nodded at the tray holding the herbal infusion and downturned her mouth.

"Yes." Elizabeth smiled. "Thank you, and some cake if Cook has any going spare."

"She baked lemon cake just yesterday."

"Perfect."

*Knock. Knock.*

"Come in," Elizabeth called.

The door opened, and her mother's lady's maid stood there. "Lady Elizabeth, Her Ladyship requests your company in the drawing room."

"She does? I told her I was having a day in my bedchamber."

"She understands that, but there is a visitor she would like you to respectfully greet."

"A visitor?" Elizabeth glanced at Sarah.

Sarah shook her head, just a little.

"Who is the visitor?" Elizabeth asked, realigning a comb and brush on her dressing table.

"It is the Duke of Farrington."

"I beg your pardon?" Her chest squeezed, and her stomach rolled some more.

"The Duke of Farrington is taking tea with Lady Burghley."

"Right now?" The words scratched over her tongue.

"Yes. Shall I tell her you'll join them shortly?"

Elizabeth picked up her perfume, a new violet scent from London, and sprayed it. She sprayed it again. Again. Again.

"Yes." Sarah rushed to her side and took the perfume. "Lady Elizabeth will be there momentarily."

Her mother's lady's maid frowned as if confused. "Certainly. Very good. I will let Her Ladyship know."

She left the room.

"But..." Elizabeth gulped and studied the door. "I can't. I just can't."

"My lady." Sarah squatted before her and took her hands. "Whatever is the matter? You have lost all your colour."

Elizabeth stared into her maid's eyes, kind eyes, understanding eyes. "I don't wish to make his acquaintance."

Those pretty blue eyes widened. "Whose acquaintance?"

"The Duke of Farrington."

"What? But...I mean, but why not? What do you know of him?"

"I've heard of him. And likely he is another suitor Mother is forcing upon me."

"And there is a problem with him?"

Elizabeth nodded as her eyes misted. "I am deeply unsure of his character."

"Is he plagued by scandal?"

"Not that I know of."

"Debt?"

"I don't believe so."

"Does he indulge in women of low morals?"

Elizabeth let out a peal of laughter. It felt good to release the emotion, but the moment she looked at Sarah's expression, she regretted it. "I would rather hope not." She straightened her face and tried to push away memories of being in his arms, his mouth on hers...his mouth on more.

"Then you should go and meet him. And if he is ugly as a toad, with rat's teeth and foul breath, then you should take your leave quickly."

Elizabeth closed her eyes and sighed. If Tom were ugly as a toad with rat's teeth and foul breath it would be easier to resist him—and if he'd come to Burghley House, he clearly had some plan that would require resisting.

She stood. Steeled herself. "No tea and lemon cake in my bedchamber, Sarah, I shall take it downstairs and be polite."

"Very good, my lady." She bowed her head. "Is there anything else I can do for you?"

"No." She paused. "Actually, yes, keep the conversation we just had private, and if you can think of an excuse to call me away soon, then please do."

"I will think of something."

"Thank you."

Elizabeth left the room and descended the staircase. Her emotions were in turmoil. Fear. Anticipation. Anger. Longing.

The man she loved was taking tea with her mother. A duke, not a gamekeeper at all. A duke.

If only things had been different. They would have been a match heaven sent.

"Ah, Elizabeth, you are here and appear well rested." Her mother beamed when Elizabeth stepped into the drawing room.

Tom stood. Riding boots and breeches gave away the fact he'd ridden to Burghley, and for once his white shirt was tucked in neatly. His cravat was perfectly tied. He dipped his head. "Lady Elizabeth."

Their eyes met. Her breath caught in her throat. His familiar features made her long for when they'd been together so easily. Painting, poetry, dreams and desires their only conversations—their only concerns.

"Will you take tea?" her mother asked.

"Yes. Thank you." She sat opposite Tom, crossed her ankles, and clasped her hands in her lap. She set her attention out of the window.

"The duke was concerned for your health," her mother said as a maid poured tea. "You disappeared so quickly after your dance with him."

"Yes, I felt quite nauseous."

"I understood it was a headache?" Tom said and raised his eyebrows at her.

She set her gaze steadily on him. "Mainly nausea if I'm honest. I get like that sometimes, all that twirling during a dance can make me quite green."

His lips tightened, and he seemed as if he was holding in words.

"But you are feeling better now?" her mother asked. "After your herbal tincture."

"Yes, thank you. In fact, I have much to do now that it has passed." She went to stand. "Do excuse me."

"No, no, dear, please sit." Her mother spoke in a tone that was not to be disobeyed.

Elizabeth sat back on the couch and reached for her cup of tea.

"The Duke of Farrington was just telling me that he has a large estate in the Highlands."

"Yes. I have only just heard about that," Elizabeth said then took a sip of tea. She looked at him over the rim.

"With many head of deer and red grouse, native only to Scotland." Her mother's tone dripped with approval.

"Very interesting." Elizabeth knew there was a note of belligerence in her tone but had been unable to keep it in check.

"You also host the fox hunt, am I right?" her mother asked Tom.

"Aye. It is quite the affair."

"Oh, so you have hounds then?" Elizabeth cocked her head. "Dogs."

He hesitated then, "Aye, I do, a substantial pack."

"You didn't mention it."

Her mother narrowed her eyes, and her jaw tightened. "Mention it?"

"When we danced," Elizabeth said, maintaining her eye contact with Tom. He knew full well what she meant. He'd had the opportunity to mention his dogs at the lodge.

"You sound interested," Tom said. "Perhaps you would like to meet my pack?"

"I hear they are not pets, the hunting hounds, quite vicious, so I'd rather not."

"You have a point. But I also own two Scotch collies, very loyal, intelligent, and friendly. You would do better to spend time with them."

"And your staff are caring for them while you are here?"

"Aye, and my sister."

"You have a sister?" Elizabeth's mother exclaimed. "How lovely."

"Gwen has not stepped out yet, she is not quite seventeen." He paused. "But the time will come."

"Another fact you didn't mention, your sister," Elizabeth said, setting her tea aside. "When we danced."

"I am very protective of her. Our mother, God rest her soul, died in childbirth with her third child; the child also didn't survive. My father..." He paused, frowned a little. "Died not long after, a broken heart some said. So it has been Gwen and I, alone, for many years, certainly for as long as she can remember." He glanced out of the window. "I have left her for too long, I must return to Kilead. She has spent some time in Edinburgh with our aunt, but her studies will soon resume with her governess at Kilead."

"I am sorry for your loss," Lady Burghley said. "Truly."

"It was a long time ago, but thank you."

"Though Kilead sounds beautiful," she went on. "A wonderful place to spend a childhood. Gwen is very lucky to have a brother like you."

"I am lucky to have her, she is a ray of sunshine on a dull day." He smiled, a wide, genuine smile. Clearly, he held a lot of affection for his sister. "And she is the other reason I have called upon you today."

"She is?" Lady Burghley asked.

"Aye. As I have told you, Kilead is beautiful, but it is remote, and I fear Gwen gets lonely even when I am there." He chuckled. "I have little to offer a conversation on gowns and hairstyles, parties and interior design. That is the domain of females, is it not?"

"Indeed." Lady Burghley laughed lightly.

The knot in Elizabeth's stomach grew tighter. The tea swirled. What was he getting at? No...not that...he wouldn't dare.

Would he?

"So I wondered." He gestured towards Elizabeth. "If Lady Elizabeth might accompany me to Kilead, with a chaperone, of course, to spend some time with Gwen."

Elizabeth's mouth fell open. It seemed he did dare. Of all the underhand, sneaky, conniving things to come up with.

"Not just for the company," he went on, "but also Beth... Lady Elizabeth's advice on the ball scene would be invaluable to my sister. She will be a debutante before I can blink twice and needing the advice and wisdom of another female." He smiled at Elizabeth. "I really would be eternally grateful."

Oh, how she wanted to slap that smile right off his face. Kilead. Her. Travel all that way with him and then have day after endless day having to see his face. That just wasn't going to happen.

No way.

"I think it's an excellent idea," her mother said.

"What?" Elizabeth snapped. "No. I can't possibly."

"I can assure you, Lady Elizabeth," Tom said, "it will all be above board and very respectful. There will be no whiff of scandal about you coming with me."

Lady Burghley laughed. "Of course it would all be most proper."

"Naturally, for I know how important that is to your daughter."

"It is," Elizabeth replied. "And...and...I simply can't go to Scotland. I have far too much to do here in Burghley."

"You do?" Her mother raised her eyebrows.

"Yes. I have more paintings to complete."

"Yet you told me..." Tom tapped the side of his head as though thinking. "That you had painted your last. Lady's orchid if I remember correctly."

He was beyond infuriating. He had an answer for everything. And where was Sarah? She was supposed to be saving her from this hellish torture.

"Yes. I have finished," she said. "So I need to be near London, for publication."

"You haven't even found a publisher yet, Elizabeth, and I'm sure this little hobby can wait." Her mother's lips tightened.

She opened her mouth to speak, but Tom got there first.

"She really is very talented from what I hear," he said. "And has amassed quite the collection of local flora paintings."

"Well, yes, you hear right." Lady Burghley frowned. "But still, I'm sure it can wait, Elizabeth."

Tom held out his palms. "And if you bring your artist's equipment we could find you some native Scottish plants to paint. That could be your second publication."

"I think not." She scowled. Her scalp itched, her chest was hot, and she'd balled her fists so hard her nails had dented her palms.

"Elizabeth." Lady Burghley's tone held a hint of scold.

"Father will never allow it, he barely knows the duke." Elizabeth pulled in a deep breath.

"That is true." Tom nodded. "But we did take a cigar together last night and discovered that we have several mutual acquaintances. I'm sure he can verify my genuine nature very quickly."

"Genuine nature," she repeated, sarcasm dripping from the words.

He smiled, almost sweetly, knowing she couldn't say more.

"I think this is an excellent plan. Scotland will be a most education-al and thrilling trip for my daughter, and I know she will be of benefit to your sister."

"Mother, what if I don't want to go?"

"You do, my dear. Yes, you do."

"I don't." Elizabeth perched on the edge of the couch. "As I said, Fa-ther will never allow it." She tipped her chin. "I am quite sure."

"If Lord Burghley has even a hint of hesitation, then there will be no more mention of it," Tom said. "That is my promise to you."

"A promise I'll hold you to." She stood. "I apologise, I feel quite un-well again, my headache and nausea has returned. Good day to you, and have a pleasant journey to Kilead."

And with that, she marched from the room. There'd be hell later from her mother, of that she was sure. Ruining her chances with an eligible duke wouldn't have gone down well. Being rude to a duke, that would get her a withering telling off.

But worth it.

Rushing into her bedchamber, she flung herself facedown on the bed and screamed into the pillow. The man was maddening. She wished she'd never met him. He'd disrupted her mind, heart, body, and soul and now was interfering in her life.

# Chapter Twelve

For the second time that day, Elizabeth stormed into her room and flung herself on the bed.

It seemed, in his wisdom, her father also thought it an excellent idea for her to go to Scotland with the duke to keep his younger sister company—with Sarah as a chaperone, of course.

She knew what both he and her mother were scheming. She had seen it in their eyes, heard it between the lines. The duke was a perfect match for her, and the sooner she wed him the better. If they could have had their way, the date would already be set.

Ha. If they knew him they wouldn't think that at all. Yes, he was handsome and charming and rich and intelligent, but he was also a man happy to be presumed as something and someone else.

She had never claimed to be a village girl, simply headed in the direction of Littlemead. Yet he had strutted, yes, that was what he'd done, strutted with his gun and a handful of game like any gamekeeper would, thoroughly acting out his role.

After yelling her frustration into the pillow, she stood and wiped her hot face, tucked her hair behind her ears, and walked to the window. Already she missed the rolling green hills of Burghley.

*How can I avoid this infernal trip?*

She racked her brains and stared out at the landscape. Maybe she could feign her headache and nausea illness was worsening. Or make up a story about a publisher in London requesting to see her work. Perhaps she could quickly get another invitation to a ball, an offer that she couldn't and shouldn't refuse. Yes, that was it. She'd start concentrating on that plan immediately.

To the right of the carriage park stood the enormous elm tree she'd played around as a child, the gnarly trunk wider than a stable door. It was in shade, owing to the heavy leaf cover. Movement caught her attention. She peered closer.

It was a horse, tied to the fence, its head dipped as it grazed. And was that...standing with the creature?

Tom, yes, it was.

In the name of the Lord, he had a nerve.

Anger heated her blood, and she gripped her gown above her ankles and marched from the room. She took the back staircase, not wanting to alert her parents he was loitering. She could and would deal with this matter.

And by the time she'd finished, she wouldn't be going to Scotland.

Striding from the house, ducking beneath a hanging vine and then skirting past a bed of parsley, she emerged onto the lawn. She was sure to stick to the shadows of a high brick wall as she made her way to the elm tree.

The horse snorted softly and swished its tail. It took no notice of her arrival.

Tom did.

He straightened and grinned that maddening grin of his. He'd removed his jacket, and his cravat was undone. He looked more like her Tom now that his attire was less formal

Her Tom. No. That he wasn't.

"What are you doing?" she snapped, standing in the cool shade of the tree and using the trunk as cover from the main house.

"I was concerned my horse had a loose shoe." He gestured vaguely in the direction of his horse's legs.

"And has it?"

"I don't think so." He shrugged and bit on his bottom lip. His gaze slipped down her body as though drinking her in.

"So," she said, her jaw tight. "Be on your way and stop...stop staring at me like that?"

"Why?"

"Because I don't like it." She lifted her chin.

"But I like looking at you. I like what I see...very much." He took a step closer. "That gown is especially fetching on you." He dropped his attention to her chest.

"Stop it, this instant." She pressed her hand to the low neckline. "I want you to go and pen a letter to my parents immediately, saying the situation has changed and I cannot accompany you to Kilead after all."

"But I want you to accompany me to Kilead." He took another pace towards her. "I desire that immensely. So why would I write such a letter?"

This time she backed up by one step. She swallowed tightly.

He came closer.

Again she retreated, until her shoulders hit the hard rough bark of the tree. Her heart was pounding. He was so damn tall looming over her, his shoulders broad and his features beguiling and familiar.

"What are you doing?" she managed.

"I am reminiscing of what it was like, when it was just you and me at the lodge. The rest of the world ceased to exist. Society ceased to exist." He paused. "You enjoyed that, too, didn't you, Beth?"

"We mustn't talk of it. Really, it was quite improper for us, a duke and a lady, to be spending so much time together without a chaperone of any kind."

"The forest was our chaperone." His face came closer. "The animals our judges."

She could see every whisker on his jawline and the small flecks of rust-brown in his otherwise green irises. "Stop."

"Stop what?"

"This."

He smiled again, his lips a little damp from where he'd just licked them. "I can't stop. You are my muse. You're all I think of, all I dream of, and all I write of."

"You are talking nonsense."

"I can assure you, I'm not."

"You need to relieve me of this trip to your estate in the Highlands."

"Why?"

"Because I don't want to go."

"Are you sure about that?" His lips very nearly brushed hers, so close she could feel the heat of them, taste his sweet breath.

"Tom. Please...stop." She gulped. Her body was betraying her. His closeness was setting off a reaction that hardened her nipples and built heat between her legs.

"I can no easier stop than the dawn can stop following night, the moon following the sun, and winter coming after summer."

She shook her head. Words piled up her mouth. They couldn't be together. They'd behaved so abominably.

"You appear dumbstruck. Is that the effect I have on you?" he asked.

"No." She set her palms on the bark, fingers spread, its scratchy surface grounding her. "You most certainly do not, but when I am around you I get this awful sense of foreboding."

"You do?" He raised his eyebrows.

"Yes. As though the scandal of us is just about to crash into the room."

"The scandal of us?" The right side of his mouth tilted as though he was amused. "I like that."

"You shouldn't. You should be ashamed of what we did."

"But why, I enjoyed it. I enjoyed kissing you, holding you, tasting your—"

"I beg you to be quiet. Someone might hear." Fear mixed with the strange longing that was gripping her belly.

"They won't." He glanced left and right. "There is only you and me under this tree. Unless you count Starlight, Gerald's favourite mare, that is. So speak freely."

"I will. Speaking freely, I ask you to unbind me from this trip that no good can come of."

"I disagree, I think a lot of good can come of it."

"Like what?"

"My sister will have female companionship. You can see a part of the world you have never seen before, paint, and I can..."

"You?"

"Can persuade you that we should be together." He touched her chin, very softly, with the tip of his finger. "You have not forgotten my proposal, I hope?"

"Your proposal was preposterous and has been dealt with."

"Dealt with?" He frowned.

"As in I said no."

He lowered his hand. His jaw tensed. "I wish to be more than a gamekeeper to you."

"You are. You are a duke who pretended to be a gamekeeper, and I want nothing to do with you since that deception."

"Stop!" He slammed his hands onto the tree, his palms slapping onto the bark either side of her head.

She started and dragged in a gasp of air. Clearly, she'd pushed him too far.

"The blame for the misunderstanding is at both of our feet." He spoke harshly.

"But I—"

"And it will not be mentioned again, do you understand?" His cheeks had reddened.

She pursed her lips together. He was angry, but what did she care? Elizabeth was angry, too. "It will only not be mentioned again when you are out of my life."

"That is not going to happen." His eyes flashed with determination.

He'd drawn his face even closer to hers. If she went on her tiptoes their noses would touch.

"You," he said, his voice low and dark and dangerous, "are going to accompany me to my home, you are going to be sweet to my sister, and we are going to spend time together as the Duke of Farrington and Lady Elizabeth, and we will do that in a civilised manner."

"And what if I refuse?" She curled her fingers against the tree. A splinter of bark dug into the pad of her right thumb.

"If you refuse." He pressed closer, his chest skimming hers, his thighs touching her legs. "Then perhaps my tongue will get looser than it has already and tell Gerald exactly what happened."

She gasped. "You wouldn't dare."

"What do you know about how daring I am? Is denying me your company in Kilead worth the risk of our sordid little secret getting out?"

"You are...you are a blackmailer on top of everything else."

"That might be." He stroked the back of his thumb down her cheek. "But I am a duke and used to getting what I want, when I want it. And the truth of the matter is, I want you, Lady Elizabeth Burghley, and I *will* have you."

She pressed her legs together, and a quiver caught her belly. His eyes mesmerised her, so did his voice. Damn, how did he have this effect on her?

"One bite of the apple," he went on with his lips almost brushing hers, "one sip of your nectar, it was not enough, not nearly enough. You have left me craving more, more of you, more of everything. I long to kiss you, hold you." He paused. "I long to put my face between your legs again and tongue your cunny until you cry out my name in pleasure and pull on my hair while you are in the grips of your ecstasy."

"Stop, please." Her throat was dry, images of what they'd done, her wanton behaviour, flashing through her mind. Her cunny was dampening at the memory. "I told you already, you can't say such lewd things. You know you can't."

"I could if you were my wife. Then we could be as lascivious as we chose in the privacy of our bedchamber."

"But that isn't going to happen." She summoned strength and pushed at his chest.

He didn't move. It was like trying to shove away the tree trunk behind her. Solid and rooted into the ground.

"Tom, let me pass."

"Not until you assure me you'll be on the carriage to the Highlands tomorrow."

"Tomorrow?"

"Aye, the sooner we leave, the sooner we are there."

"But it is so far, I need to prepare." She pushed at him again, still with no success. "There is much to do before such an excursion."

"I am sure you will manage, you have many gowns and shawls, as any lady does."

"But what about...? Oh, just let me pass."

"Say you are coming with me."

An infuriating knot formed in her stomach. She grunted with frustration and screwed up her face.

"Beth?"

"Oh, all right. I will come. But not because I want to but because you have left me no choice."

"That's right." He stepped aside. "You have no choice but to come with me." He reached for his horse's reins and pulled up her head. "But I can assure you, Lady Elizabeth, you will have a splendid time and want for nothing. Satisfaction is guaranteed."

And with that, he threw himself up on the horse, and without bothering to stirrup his feet, dug his heels into the creature's flanks and took off at a gallop on the grass alongside the driveway.

"You are such a..." She shook her fist at him and then gave in and stamped her foot which she'd wanted to do during the entire conversation. "Pain in the rear end, Tom."

Satisfaction guaranteed. What on earth was he talking about?

# Chapter Thirteen

Elizabeth was weary. They'd been travelling since early morning, and now the sun was slipping from the dusky sky. Her back ached, and her belly was rumbling.

"Would you like this, my lady?" Sarah asked, offering her a blue woollen blanket.

"Yes, thank you." She took it, set it on her knees, and looked out of the window again. The hot brick beneath her feet was cooling.

"We will soon rest for the night. At the Border Inn," Tom said.

She nodded curtly. She'd spent the entire day avoiding conversation with Tom who sat opposite her, but thankfully a little to the right so she hadn't got as bad a creak in her neck as she could have.

"The food at the inn has been most agreeable on my previous visits," he went on. "We will likely dine on lamb, and I'm sure I will be able to source a decent wine or port."

"I will dine in my room." She risked a glance at him.

He was holding his notebook and quill. All day he'd been jotting down words, or poems, she wasn't sure which.

He raised his eyebrows slightly. "As you wish, Lady Elizabeth."

Sarah remained quiet. She'd only spoken when spoken to on the journey, which is what was expected of her.

"You will notice out of the window," Tom said, "the landscape has changed. The hills are taller, steeper, there is an abundance of woodland, and you may well feel a chill in the air sooner than at home."

She pressed her lips together. Home was where she wanted to be.

Soon, they came to the inn. The carriage drew to a halt, and the horses neighed in apparent relief.

"Ah good." Tom didn't wait for the footman to open the door. He hopped out and held his hand to Elizabeth.

She had no choice but to take it, the drop to the ground was substantial, and she placed her gloved fingers on his palm. As she alighted, he held her tight and supported her elbow to stop her unbalancing.

"Thank you," she said stiffly. Though when he released her, she could still feel his touch. A patch of heat that sent small waves of sensation up and down her arm.

It appeared no matter how cunning he'd been to get his own way, and a day of being as cool as ice with him, her body still betrayed her—still was drawn to his.

If it had been ladylike to curse as they went into the inn, she would have.

"If you change your mind," Tom said, "I'll be beside the fire." He smiled congenially, as if there was not a hint of frostiness between them.

She'd found that was more maddening than if they'd been arguing.

He had a breaking point, though, she'd discovered that under the elm tree. Perhaps she'd find it again and he'd release her from this blasted trip and send her home.

"This is a nice room," Sarah said, opening Elizabeth's case.

"It will suffice." It was in the eves, but the roof was high and the window large. Right now it glowed red as the sun sent a final blast of energy over the horizon.

"Ah good, there is warm water," Sarah said. "Here is your soap, my lady."

"Thank you." Elizabeth slipped off her shawl and shoes and went to the washbasin. She freshened up.

Sarah moved around the room, humming and sorting Elizabeth's clothes for the next day of travel and then turned down the bed.

Elizabeth was glad of her. Sarah was her only ally in this escapade.

"Appears very clean, no bed bugs," Sarah said. "The duke picked a good inn for us to rest in."

"At least that is something." She dried her face then sat on the stool at a dresser.

Sarah stepped up behind her and immediately began to unpin Elizabeth's hair. "You do not wish to go to Kilead, my lady?"

Elizabeth looked at her maid in the mirror. "Do you?"

"Oh yes." She nodded enthusiastically. "I have only ever been to the village and the Burghley Estate. Once I nearly travelled to Cottonbridge, to run an errand, but that never happened."

Elizabeth was quiet. She couldn't imagine only ever having been to two places in all of her life. They were the same age, she and Sarah, or at least she thought as much. "I'm sorry, you should have accompanied me to London a time or two."

"You have no need for me there, my lady, you have a full house of staff."

"That is true, but perhaps when this trip is over, we could arrange for you to come one time. So you can experience the ton."

"Thank you, my lady." She paused. "Cook said that Scotland is cold, that they all talk funny. But I don't think the duke talks funny, do you?" She paused. "Well, maybe a bit."

"He talks too much." Elizabeth frowned.

"He writes a lot, too, don't you think?" Sarah dropped a collection of pins on the dresser and reached for a bone-handled comb. She set to work on Elizabeth's hair. "In his notepad."

"I didn't notice."

"I did. All day, he kept writing a few words here and there, not that I could read them. I can't read, can I, my lady. But he seemed quite intent on it and..."

"Go on."

"I got the feeling he was writing about you."

"Why would you think that?"

"His gaze was on you constantly, as if he can't get enough of looking at you, as though...no, I shouldn't say it."

"Pray do."

"He seems mesmerised by you, fascinated, his eyes get a softness when they're set on you."

Elizabeth huffed. "I doubt that very much."

Sarah was quiet for a minute, working on a knot, then, "He is not as ugly as a toad as we feared; in fact, he is very handsome, tall, too, and very well presented."

Elizabeth thought back to how he'd presented himself in the forest. Half naked, his torso slick with sweat as he chopped logs, his breeches scuffed with dirt, and his hair messily pushed back from his face.

Her stomach clenched, and she closed her eyes. The memory of being in his arms, primitive, drunk on desire, captured by his essence. It was not something she could forget.

It was something she ought to forget. And so should he.

"You do not think him handsome?" Sarah asked.

"He is...passable." Elizabeth stood, her hair had been combed enough. "But I don't wish to spend my evening talking about him. I intend to read my book, if you could organise some supper to be sent to my room."

"Of course, my lady." Sarah placed the comb down. "I will go straight to the kitchen."

She left the room, and Elizabeth sat on the bed with a sigh. Sarah was right, of course, the duke was very handsome, strong, too, and clearly a fine huntsman and horse rider. He was also very determined, and stubborn, and talented. A man whose presence could not be ignored because he had a wicked, seductive glint in his eye and a dark tone in his voice...on occasion...that made sin sound sweeter than honey.

If only they'd met at a ball. Stepped out. Behaved as the aristocrats they were instead of acting like rampant beasts in the forest.

*Knock. Knock.*

She turned to the door.

"Who is it?"

No answer.

Standing, she walked to it and carefully opened it a crack. "What are you doing here?"

"I have a present for you," Tom said.

"You can't be here with me unchaperoned, it's quite scandalous and...oh—"

He pushed in. "No one knows us at The Border Inn."

"I beg to differ." She rolled her eyes. "Sarah."

"Sarah is listening to gossip in the kitchen." He held out a book. "Here, I want you to have this."

"What is it?"

"You can see what it is." He shifted from one foot to the other and knotted his fingers together. Bit on his bottom lip.

There was something almost vulnerable about the gesture, and she peered curiously at the title of the book, wondering what had thrown his confidence, even if just by a hair's breadth.

"*Poems from the Highlands* by T Kilead. Volume One." She paused. "T Kilead. Is this you? A pen name?"

"Aye." He swallowed, the sound noisy in the quiet room. "Not terribly anonymous or creative, but it's what I went with."

"You...you're published? Your poems are published?" She flicked open the hard cover and scanned page after page of delicate printed script. "Why didn't you tell me? This is amazing. I'm impressed."

"Would you have believed me?"

"As a gamekeeper...perhaps not." She smiled and shook her head. What an achievement. "But as the Duke of Farrington, yes, I would have." She closed the book. "You seem pretty capable of anything you put your mind to."

"I've signed this copy." He tapped it. "And I want you to read it. Well, if you *want* to that is. Poetry isn't for everyone and—"

"I will read it. Thank you." She felt the weight of it. It was satisfyingly heavy.

"My publisher is waiting on volume two," he said, walking to the window and drawing the curtains. "That was the reason I was at Pheasant Lodge."

She waited for him to go on.

"I was struggling to find inspiration in Scotland. I'd hit a brick wall. It was as if all the emotions I have about my homeland had gushed out of me in volume one and there was nothing left to say. Not that I don't love the Highlands, I do, but I'd said what I wanted to. And then..."

"And then...?"

"Then Gerald suggested isolation and nature, stripping everything away. I took him up on his offer to use Pheasant Lodge." He paused. "Still nothing was coming to me, and just as I was about to give up hope, head for home, you showed up."

She folded her arms, studied the width of his shoulders as he stared at the closed curtains. His jacket was dark; the tails hung over his breeches covering his behind.

"I saw you," he said quietly, "by the lake. A beautiful vision of purity, femininity, almost ethereal, and from that moment on the words came to me, the words, emotions, I was possessed by the hunger to write again." He turned. "Write about you."

"I'm flattered."

"Don't be. It's not about that. It's because you've touched me here." He pressed his chest. "That's why I am writing again."

His words chipped away a corner of the ice around her heart. "You saw me? At the lake?"

"Aye. I was sitting quietly, and you came and paddled."

"And you didn't make yourself known."

"For that I am sorry. But by the time I'd come to my senses," he smiled a little, "you were paddling and clearly believed to be alone, and

I didn't know how to introduce myself without startling you...without you thinking I'd been spying."

She nodded slowly. "I see."

"So I left, went back to the lodge, and then you came along, again, and by then I was already writing about you. In fact, it will be the first poem in volume two."

"What is the title?"

"'My Beautiful Nymph.'"

"Nymph." She couldn't help but smile. "A spirit, a woodland maiden, that is what you thought I was."

"It's how I saw you." He paused. "You'll be the first to read it."

"Thank you." She inclined her head. "You should go, before Sarah catches you here confessing to watching me when I thought I was alone."

"I should." He stepped closer. "And I will if..."

"What?"

"It would be nice to have some conversation in the carriage tomorrow. We have a long day ahead."

"Perhaps that..." She looked up at him. "Depends on how well entertained I am by this book." She held it between them.

He chuckled. "That is a deal. Though you know I won't sleep a wink now."

"I am sure you will sleep quite well."

He tipped his head closer still. Like before, the rest of the world seemed to recede, the bedchamber becoming the only place in the world.

"I would sleep better," he whispered, "with a wife in my arms."

Her belly tightened. "I am sure you will have a wife, one day."

He breathed deep, as though inhaling the scent of her jasmine soap. "You're right. I will."

As suddenly as he'd arrived, he was gone, slipping from the room and leaving behind a coil of emotion in Elizabeth.

She held the book to her chest and closed her eyes. She was trying to stay angry with him, but he was making that pretty hard when he had brought her poetry.

She thought back to that afternoon at the lake. Remembered hearing a twig snap and thinking that it was a creature, a deer perhaps. All along it had been Tom, watching her, his creativity beginning to flow again, his inspiration sparking.

Had a woman ever been wooed in such a manner? Then fallen for one person who turned out to be another? Had a lady ever been borrowed from her family home and taken to the remote Highlands? She didn't think so. One thing was for certain, the Duke of Farrington was a curious man who she didn't think she'd ever get bored of learning more about.

At that thought she became irritated once again. How was it he strung her emotions up like clothing on a washing line? He was easier to understand when he was a gamekeeper, living a simple life in the forest. Now...now she had to see through layers to get to the real him.

She sat and opened the book. The inside cover held his neat, feathery writing.

*To my muse, a beautiful woman with many layers, all of which I hope to, one day, uncover. T Kilead.*

She tensed, and her heart squeezed. He thought the same of her. Layers.

# Chapter Fourteen

They set off in a rainstorm. Wrapped in a shawl and blanket, Elizabeth sat with her gloved hands clasped and her bonnet pulled tight. She was pale, and slight rings sat beneath her eyes. Tired perhaps? Weary at the thought of another long day rattling along in the carriage.

Tom worried about her and wished the rain and wind would push east and give her a view of the Highlands as they began to make their way through them, but it seemed Mother Nature had other ideas. The hurrying mist swirled, a pale, inky fog that blustered and bounced over the dips and troughs of the meadows and fields the track was cutting through.

"Here, take a lemon drop, Lady Elizabeth," he said, offering forward a small paper bag.

"Thank you." She took one, popped it in her mouth then closed her eyes, seeming to signal she didn't want to talk.

He offered Sarah a sweet treat. She took one happily and returned to watching the blustery weather through the small window.

Tom was content to suck a lemon drop and study Beth. She was a curiosity, that was for sure. He never knew what mood or emotion was going to tumble from her. And far from that being irritating, he found it fascinating.

He'd known her to be a perfect vision, an inquisitive mind, a determined artist, a passionate woman, angry, frustrated, stubborn. Last night he'd seen new glints in her eyes, when he'd given her the poetry book and confessed to why he had been at Pheasant Lodge and that he'd watched her from afar.

Had she been placated by his admission? Her obvious anxiety about what they'd done eased somewhat by his honesty?

He didn't know. He could only hope so. And as he'd predicted, he'd barely slept a wink for wondering what she would think of his poems, and if she would indeed indulge in conversation with him on the remainder of their journey.

"I am hesitant to ask, Lady Elizabeth," he said when he could stand it no longer. "But did you read any of the book I gave you?"

She opened her eyes and gave him a steady stare.

His heart did a weird flip, one it always did when an opinion was coming about his work.

"Yes." She twisted her mouth as if in thought. "I did."

He swallowed. "And?"

"It was an interesting message to the recipient."

He chuckled. "That is what you wish to discuss?"

"You believe a person has layers?"

"We are all layered, are we not?"

She didn't answer, so he went on.

"There is the top layer shown to society, the polite conversation, adherence to correct conduct. It is a polished layer shown in the way we move at balls, through the ton, at business meetings."

A slight frown formed between her eyebrows.

"And then there are the private layers of a person, Lady Elizabeth, the layers that hold hopes and dreams, fears and desires."

"Can a person not discuss hopes and dreams in society?"

"Aye, some of them." He paused. "But some are for sharing with the people they are closest to. People they love and trust." He leaned forward. "And some layers, the deepest ones, right at the core of a person, are only to be shared with one other person in all of the world." His voice dropped. "These layers are bright with passion but also marred with vulnerability. It is in the core that love is born, but with love comes the possibility of being hurt and rejected, the very soul broken."

She licked her lips, coating them in a slight sheen.

He longed to kiss her, taste the sugary lemon he was sure would be there. A flush of awareness went through his belly, to his groin, and he had to push away a memory of them embracing in the lodge, how she'd felt in his arms, the way her tongue had stroked against his.

"And is this what volume two will be about?" she asked, still studying him.

"It will be about many emotions." He smiled, hoping to extract one from her. "Because right now, I feel like my emotions are flying high. I am feeling things I have never felt before."

Sarah glanced his way. She looked about to say something, but instead quickly returned her attention to the window.

"Well, I hope for your sake," Elizabeth said, "that the words flow easily. For the first volume was indeed quite spectacular, and I'm sure your readers will be excitedly anticipating more."

"Spectacular!" He beamed. "Really? That is what you thought?"

Her frown deepened. "Yes. In truth, I feel like I have already been to the Highlands. Your poignant descriptions are simply wonderful."

"You, Lady Elizabeth, have just made my day, heck, no, make that my week." He paused. "Are you being serious?"

"Deadly." She gestured out of the window. "Though it is somewhat of a shame I can't see the Highlands for myself."

"Oh, but you will. I promise you that." He pressed his hand to his chest. "I will show you moors, and waterfalls, and stags and eagles, everything. We will walk, we will walk to the top of Eagle Point. I will take you."

"It all sounds so exotic and wonderful," Sarah blurted. She clasped her hands. "I can't wait to see the Highlands, I simply can't."

Tom laughed. "Well, you must wait, Sarah, for a few more hours, but I do believe there is a break in the clouds." He pointed out of the window. "There, see."

Both ladies peered at the parting in the clouds. Behind it was a brilliant flash of blue over a pointed mountain tip.

He sensed Beth's mood lighten. It was the way she sat up a little straighter, her eyes suddenly glistening with the prospect of new adventures.

He'd been right to insist she accompany him. "When we arrive," he said, encouraged, "we will warm beside the fire and eat venison and drink whisky made in my own distillery."

"I am unsure if whisky is a drink for me," she said with a small smile.

"Ah, but you haven't tasted this one." He pressed his fingers to his lips as though kissing them. "It is simply divine, so smooth it is like syrup, and it has spent months in oak barrels, and the taste of the wood, it is there, a subtle stroke of your tongue like walking in the forest and breathing deep, actually tasting the trees around you."

She nodded slowly, and he wondered what she was thinking about—the whisky, the forest, or the stroke of his tongue.

"You make me long to be at Kilead..." Elizabeth paused as the carriage jolted in and out of a particularly large pothole. "Which I never thought I'd say."

* * * *

Finally, they rattled through Kilead's huge iron gates, past the gatekeeper's cottage, and started on the mile-long drive to the main house. Night was rapidly creeping up, the horses had needed to be changed twice, and Sarah had been sleeping for over two hours.

"Home," Tom said, almost to himself. "At last."

"Will I meet Gwen tonight?" Beth asked.

"If she has returned from Edinburgh, aye."

"What? I thought she was here already? I thought she was lonely and in need of female company. Isn't that the whole point of me coming to Kilead?"

"Of course. Of course." He popped his notebook and quill into the bag with the lemon drops. "And I'm sure she will arrive very soon."

"So you *know* she is not here?"

"How can I know for sure when I have been away for many weeks?"

"Tom...I mean...you...this is..." She clenched her gloved hands and frowned. "You are infuriating, you know that?"

"And good at getting my own way. You have to give me credit on that front." He couldn't hold in a grin.

"And sneaky and conniving." She waggled her finger at him. "If your sister is not here, I am turning this carriage around and heading straight back to Burghley."

"We will see."

"What does that mean?"

"It means we will see...if she is here."

"You are talking in riddles now." She folded her arms, clearly thoroughly frustrated with him.

And she had good reason to be.

His sister wasn't at Kilead. She had likely another week in Edinburgh with their aunt. But Beth wasn't going anywhere, not now he had her here, at least not until she admitted that what they'd had together was special. Those stolen moments in the forest when no one else had existed, and neither of them had titles, or inheritances, or responsibilities. Those moments had been more than special. They'd been the essence of man and woman, the meaning of life, the reason they'd been put on Earth.

The carriage drew to a stop, and this time he waited for a footman with an umbrella to assist Beth to the shelter of the portcullis.

When he alighted he quickly joined her, then stretched out his arms and back, let out a groan. As ever, it was a relief to have the journey from England over with.

The door opened. Two dogs ran out, black and tan with what looked like fluffy white beards. They barked wildly and ran in circles around Tom.

"Hey, you fellas," he said, ruffling their heads. "Lady Elizabeth, this is Arne and Shiled."

"Welcome home," a butler said smiling.

"Hamish, thank you." Tom squeezed his shoulder. "Good to see you. Everything in order?"

"Perfect order, your grace." He nodded.

"Did we get many hound puppies? When I left there were a few expected."

"Twenty-one in total."

"That is a good result." Tom grinned.

"We are glad to have you back, and just before nightfall at that."

"I am happy to be here. This is Lady Elizabeth. She will be keeping Lady Gwen company."

"But—?"

"If you could..." Tom pointed outside. The two dogs were running in circles around the carriage. "Lady Elizabeth's lady's maid, Sarah, is helping with the luggage. Perhaps you could find her some assistance, then she will need to be given staff accommodation and fed. It has, as always, been a long journey."

"Of course. I will see that Sarah is quite comfortable. It will be nice to have a fresh wee face around here."

"That is what I thought." Tom gestured into the grand entrance hall. "This way, Lady Elizabeth."

Elizabeth walked beside him, her head sweeping from left to right as she took in the vast room. Burghley House was magnificent, but Kilead was magnificently Scottish, and the entrance lit by an imposing candelabra that hung from a black beam was currently looking its best.

The stonework was exposed, the floor and sweeping staircase dark oak, and the polished lintels above each doorway decorated with brass ornaments. The wall to the west had a large, arched stained-glass window depicting the image of mountains and shepherds, and opposite hung taxidermy heads of stags, foxes, wolves, and boars. Beneath them, a vast glass cabinet awash with swords, daggers, shields, and rifles.

"This is..." She pointed upwards. The ceiling was five storeys high, owing to the fact the centre of the house was a vacuous turret. "I've never seen anything like it. It's...it's a castle."

"Aye, it is, but quite habitable, I assure you."

"And this is where you grew up?"

"Aye. Look, that portrait is of my parents." He nodded at a huge oil painting of his father and mother both decked out in plaids of the family tartan. Behind them, the Highlands dominated the landscape, an impressive stag staring out from beside a lake.

"It is a remarkable painting," she said. "And they are a very handsome couple."

"They were good and kind parents, I miss them every day." He raised his hand at Hamish. "Could you please see that Lady Elizabeth is shown to her room, the loch view room in the east wing."

"Very good, your grace." Hamish nodded.

Tom took Beth's hand and drew her knuckles to his lips. "I will see you shortly for supper."

And then he'd have to confirm that his sister wasn't home. That news wasn't likely to go down well.

# Chapter Fifteen

Elizabeth slipped off her shoes and walked over a large sheepskin rug. It must have been four or five hides sewn together and was deliciously soft on her stockinged soles.

Next to the rug was a canopied bed—her bed for the duration of her visit which she felt entitled to cut very short should Gwen not be at Kilead. The bed's canopy was deep red with long drapes held back by thick golden swags. Beside it sat a fireplace, the back and chimney-breast licked with soot, the hearth stacked high with kindling. Several fat, lit candles flickered on the mantel.

It was a big room, but still cosy, owing to the dark wood panelled walls and the thickly gilded frames around the landscape paintings, of which there were many. The window had three aspects, two small side panels of glass and a larger one looking out at the shadowed mountains, and a tartan cushioned window seat. Beside the window, a table held a stack of books and a statue of a long-horned bull with shaggy fur.

Hamish had assured her a maid would arrive presently to pull the curtains, light the fire, and draw her a bath. Sarah would also soon arrive to help her settle in and prepare for dinner.

Elizabeth ran her finger over a shiny dressing table. On it sat several framed paintings. They were all of children, a young boy and girl. Were they Tom and Gwen? It was hard to know. A small mother of pearl jewellery tray glistened in the wavering light.

An open door to the right of the bed showed her it was a wash-room, her washroom, complete with tub, and a door opposite, tucked behind a modesty screen decorated with images of storks and reeds, was slightly ajar.

*What is through there?*

She ducked behind the screen and peered through the gap between door and frame which was no wider than two of her fingers.

From what she could see, this room was almost identical to hers in mirror image. The shadows were long, the fire already lit and sending its noisy crackles and a whiff of smoke her way. It was unusual that the adjoining door was open, if someone was using the next door bedchamber.

And that someone was Tom.

He strode into her line of vision, stripping off his shirt as he walked and slinging it to the bed.

She gasped and stepped back, drawing her fingers to her lips. Her heart did a weird little flip. She shouldn't have seen that.

But it had hardly been her fault.

She gulped and looked again.

He was stooped now, beside the bed, peeling off his boots and socks. His shoulders were as tan and broad as she remembered, his back long and lean, and the muscles in his arms tensed and flexed as he moved.

Her mouth dried, and her belly clenched. He was the most handsome man she'd ever seen.

He straightened, hooked his hands into the waistband of his breeches, and pushed.

*I have to turn away.*

But she couldn't. Elizabeth was utterly stuck in place, as though her feet had been sewn to the floor. She held her breath and her eyes widened.

In one swift movement, he removed his last item of clothing. The dark-brown fan of hair that ran from his navel thickened as it reached his groin. His flaccid cock was thick and long, as big as she remembered it being from that one time when he'd...when they'd...

Her lungs heated. Still she kept her breath trapped.

He put his hands over his head again, something he was fond of doing after sitting, and stretched. His torso elongated, and the tendons in his neck were taut as he tipped his head back and his strong, hair-coated legs tensed.

And then suddenly, he dropped his arms to his sides, let out a big sigh, and stepped out of her view.

Oh dear Lord.

She turned and closed her eyes, his image still burning into her mind. Finally letting out her breath, she hugged herself. A myriad of sensations played her body as though it were a musical instrument. She felt tight, tingling, energised, excited, alert, desperate, aching...

How could one man be so beautiful, so perfect? Was it this feeling that made artists pick up their brushes before a human subject? Were these emotions simply a longing to be creative?

Perhaps she should paint some figures, maybe then she'd get a handle on this ludicrous longing to touch Tom, stroke her fingertips over his chest, his abdomen, lower still. Learn his physique the way she learnt the shapes of leaves, petals, and stamen.

Yes, that is what she would do. It would surely help. She'd begin drawing people, lay to rest this curiosity with the human form.

"My lady, I am sorry to keep you waiting?" Sarah rushed into the bedchamber.

Quickly, Elizabeth stepped out from behind the screen. Sarah was concentrating on manoeuvring two heavy leather trunks.

"It is quite all right." She swallowed tightly; thank goodness she hadn't been caught spying.

"I will light the fire, my lady." A young chambermaid scooted to the fire and squatted before it.

"Hot water is on the way for you to bathe," Sarah said. "I trust that is what you want."

"Very much so." She smiled and took a deep breath. Was Tom at this very moment lowering his naked body into a tub of deep, warm, scented water? Did his bones ache from the journey? Was he as weary as she?

Only she didn't feel as weary now she'd peeped through his door. Something in her felt alive and peculiarly hungry...but not for food.

The fire caught, grasping flames stretching upwards like arms reaching into the chimney. The tub was being filled—clearly there was a servant's door into the washroom.

"What would you like to wear for supper tonight?" Sarah asked, opening the first of Elizabeth's trunks.

"The dark-blue gown, with the black embroidery on the front panel."

"Very good, my lady." Sarah quickly found it and laid it on the bed. She then rushed into the washroom. "No, no, not rose, Lady Burghley likes jasmine. Wait, I'll get it. No, actually, you have done enough, thank you, please leave us."

"Aye, thank you."

The quiet click of a door, then, "My lady, your tub is ready."

Elizabeth glanced over the screen at the top of the door. A scratch of light came in from the adjacent room. What if Tom were to watch her undress? Would he enjoy that? Would he be so bold? Would he stay silent again or would he march into the room, confident, aroused, determined, and take her right there and then? Give her the pleasure he had at Pheasant Lodge. Have her gasping his name, dragging on his hair, clutching him to her with her bent legs.

A small tremble of longing started in her groin and went up her back, over her scalp then settled in her chest, a dense weight of need.

A need for Tom.

"My lady." Sarah appeared. "It is ready."

"Thank you. Of course. Yes." She strode to the washroom, her undergarments a little damp and her nipples tingling. Infuriating as the Duke of Farrington was, he'd certainly wormed his way into her secret thoughts.

\* \* \* \*

"How was your venison?" Tom asked, setting his cutlery down.

"Excellent." She smiled and finished the last bite.

"And the port sauce?"

"A perfect accompaniment." And she meant it. The sauce had been divine. "You clearly have a very skilled cook here at Kilead." She lay her knife and fork on the plate which was patterned with the Kilead tartan around the edge.

"Aye, Mrs MacDougal is the best. When I'm away from home, after a while, I begin to crave her pigeon pie, and also the way she cooks ox tongue with onions and herbs and these tiny sage dumplings." He smiled. "Just delicious."

"Was she the cook here when you were a child?"

"Aye, that she was."

"So they are all the flavours of your childhood?"

"I suppose they are." He gestured to two soft seats beside a roaring fire. The fire was set in a solid marble fireplace, the mantel held a large wooden clock with a brass face and above it, on the stone wall, a silver shield bearing the image of an eagle. "Shall we sit for an after dinner tipple? I am longing for you to try the estate whisky."

"Yes, though it is getting late."

"Of course. I am sorry, you are weary."

"There is that." She stood from her seat at the dining table and flattened the front of her gown to remove a crease. "Also that I haven't met your sister yet? I thought she might join us for supper. Surely she will be retiring soon."

"Ah, about Gwen." He came to her side, cupped her elbow, and steered her to the chair on the left.

A servant began clearing away their plates. The dogs looked up from their position by the fire, clearly wondering if there'd be scraps.

"No begging." Tom wagged his finger at them. Both put their heads down again.

"About Gwen?" Elizabeth said firmly and sat and rested her hands on her lap.

"Bring us whisky," Tom said to the servant. "Two good measures of my last opened bottle, that was a good year."

"Aye, your grace, right away."

He sat, curled his hands over the arm of the chair, and smiled at her. The fire cast one side of his face in near darkness.

"Your sister?" Elizabeth pressed.

"Aye, it seems she sent message to Kilead to confirm she wouldn't be returning for a few days?"

"Mmm, I see." Elizabeth sighed.

"I am sorry, I can tell that you are disappointed."

"I am disappointed not that Gwen isn't here, but that you lied to me, Tom."

"Lied?" He pressed his chest. "I am sorry you think that, but it is not true."

"Is it not?"

He dipped his head. "I'll confess I was not positive she would be here on our arrival, but I did believe she would be close behind us if she were not. And that, Beth, is true."

"We will wait and see."

He leaned forward. "I really do apologise, but I can't deny I wanted you here, and sooner rather than later." He frowned and shook his head. "I wanted you here with me. I told you at Pheasant Lodge I wanted you. Is that so terrible? So unforgivable? To want you?"

"Your whisky, your grace." Hamish appeared with a silver tray holding two crystal glasses containing deep amber liquid and a half-full decanter.

"Ah, here we go." Tom took one, apparently at ease with Hamish having caught the end of what he'd been saying.

"Swirl it a wee bit, then smell it." Tom held the glass up then rotated it until the drink waved just below the rim.

She took a glass and watched him. His conversation had rushed on, conveniently, now the whisky had arrived.

*Is it so bad that he still wants me? That his feelings haven't changed?*

"And then, Beth, taste it. Savour it. Rejoice in it." He brought the glass to his lips, sipped, then closed his eyes. "Ahh...you will truly know you are in the Highlands."

Elizabeth did the same. The flavour was intense, but it didn't grow. Instead, her mouth bloomed warm and peaty, smoky almost. She, too, closed her eyes.

"What do you think?" he asked.

"It's strong, unusual, but I like it." She looked at him again.

"Good, for I have an entire cellar full of barrels." He laughed. "You can have as much as you want." He nodded at Hamish. "That will be all, thank you. Just leave the decanter."

"Very good, your grace."

"I don't think I should have too much." Elizabeth didn't have to be a whisky expert to know it was a very strong drink. "Can I ask you a question?"

"On one condition. He crossed his right ankle over his left knee and settled back. The half-grin on his face was maddening, sexy and intriguing.

"A condition?"

"Aye."

"And what is that condition, Tom?"

# Chapter Sixteen

"You will take a walk with me tomorrow," Tom said, "around the estate. I long to show you it. The plant life here, at this time of year will take your breath away, I am certain of it. For I know how much you admire, and what an expert you are with all things flora."

"It is true I am intrigued to see new plants." Elizabeth paused. "So yes, with a chaperone, I would like to see your estate."

"A chaperone?" He raised his eyebrows and took a sip of his drink.

"Yes, a chaperone." She, too, sipped. It really was very good. "So if I may ask you now, if you don't mind, how old was Gwen when you lost your parents?"

He glanced away, the corners of his mouth drooped slightly. "She was just three years old when Mother died, three and six months when I buried our father."

"Which made you how old, Tom?"

"Fifteen."

"Gosh, so young." She studied him. He'd had so much on his shoulders from such a tender age.

"Young but perfectly capable. I'd watched my father manage the running of the estate for years. I was home-schooled, my parents liked it that way, so when I wasn't studying I was horseback riding to check on the gamekeepers, the deer herd, the sheep, the boundaries, and in the winter months my father showed me how to keep books, how to balance the finances coming in and going out." He paused. "They were happy times."

"I am truly sorry for your loss." She drained her drink, emotions squeezing her chest. "It must have been lonely here, when you lost them."

"I can't deny that there have been lonely times, but I am wealthy not just in land but also in friends. Gerald is a great chap, he's spent many a summer here with me."

131

"Where did you meet?"

"Through our parents, our fathers did business."

"I see."

"And the staff here at Kilead." He paused. "Perhaps a wee bit different to Burghley because they are also my friends. We are so remote here, cut off in the winter for many weeks due to the weather, so we're all we have."

"Really? Cut off?"

"Aye, the Highlands are not for the fainthearted, and also not for one man alone. Folk have to stick together." He smiled suddenly and looked upwards. "No man is an island. Entire of itself. Every man is a piece of the continent. A part of the main."

"One of yours?"

"I wish." He chuckled and stood, reached for the decanter. "It is John Donne. I like the sentiment, mankind is as one."

"I like that, too."

He topped up her empty glass.

"So tell me also," she said, "for it sounds as though you managed Kilead well from a young age, how did you manage being a big brother as well as surrogate parent?"

"Ah, that..." He sat, sipped. "Was not something my father had trained me for."

"Was he a good father?"

"Very. Kind, patient, always wanted me to do my best. I knew he loved me."

She smiled. "And have you always been kind and patient with Gwen? Let her know you love her?"

"I suppose I have." He nodded slowly. "Aye."

"So you did learn from your father."

He was quiet for a moment, then, "You are very wise, you know that."

She laughed. "I'm only saying what I see."

"Which is how you paint. Recreating exactly what you see." He paused. "You know my publisher in Edinburgh might be interested in your work. I hear illustrated publications are proving very popular at the moment, and yours are exceptional."

"Really?" She leant forward. "Do you think so?"

He nodded. "Perhaps I will get the opportunity to introduce you, if you stay at Kilead long enough."

"Mmm," she sat back. "I fear this is another ruse, this time not to get me here but to keep me here."

He laughed, his eyes sparkling. "And what sane man with hot blood running through his veins wouldn't want you by his side for as long as possible?"

"I am here to keep your sister company, remember."

"And since she is not here, I get to keep *you* company." He stood and topped up her drink again.

"Oh, no, I really shouldn't." Her head was feeling a little light, her limbs heavy.

He stopped pouring. He'd only delivered the tiniest mouthful, and instead splashed liquid into his own glass. He sat. "When we take a turn around the estate tomorrow, I wish to show you the rutting stags, they are quite spectacular. Perhaps, if we're lucky, we'll spot a golden eagle." He gestured to the shield above the fire. "The creature on our family crest."

"I have never seen an eagle."

"You will be most impressed, the wing span alone is a sight." He paused, chewed on his bottom lip.

She stared at it, remembering what his lips felt like pressing down on hers. Soft yet strong, eager but gentle, and his arms around her, a warm safe embrace that allowed her to give in to herself, to her desires, her needs.

Dragging in a breath, she sat up straighter. What was she doing thinking along these lines? "I really ought to turn in." She nodded at the clock. The hour was late. "I am very tired."

"As am I." He stood. "But the long journey is over now."

She nodded. "Please sit. I will find my own way to the bedchamber."

"Are you sure?"

"Of course, we are not out in the wild Highlands now but in your home."

"And I hope you make yourself at home."

She nodded and held in a hiccup. "I bid you good night, Tom."

"And I you." He smiled. A devilishly handsome smile that weakened her knees, and they were already a little shaky.

After opening the heavy door, she stepped out into the vast entrance hall. She looked up at the stained-glass window. The images appeared to merge together in the candlelight, and she blinked and turned away.

The staircase was much wider and much longer than she remembered, and she held up the hem of her gown with one hand and the bannister with the other as she climbed them. The painted eyes of Tom's ancestors seemed to follow her, and when she reached the top, she took a quick right turn and scooted past a suit of armour holding a spear, and a glass box containing a stuffed white fox.

The corridor ahead was dark with only one stubby candle flickering on a wrought-iron sconce. She hurried along, took another right and then a left, her way lit now by a high window spilling in moonlight.

Where was her bedchamber? Surely it was the next door. She'd come this way before, with Hamish...hadn't she?

Pushing her way into the first room she came to, she was instantly hit with the musty scent of dustsheets. She came to a halt in a patch of moonlight pouring in from a vast window.

This was a bedchamber, but not hers.

The bed was stripped of linen, and on it sat a stone foot warmer. Around it, like angular ghosts, furniture was covered in large white sheets. Another suit of armour stood by the window, next to it a stack of four tea chests stamped with red numbers.

"Where am I?" she muttered, slowly turning and taking in the room. A huge tapestry hung on the wall, and a neatly swept fireplace lay dormant.

"My parents' room."

She started at Tom's deep voice suddenly behind her. "Oh." She pressed her hand to her chest, her heart beating fast. "You scared me."

"I'm sorry." He came a little closer, stepping into her beam of moonlight. "I had a feeling you would get lost. Kilead can be a maze."

"Yes, it can." She glanced around. "I am sorry, to have unwittingly come in here."

"It is not a problem." He shrugged. "I should have moved myself in here after their deaths, but I preferred to keep the room I'd grown up in."

"I can understand that."

"And it has taken me years to go through their personal possessions." He gestured to the tea boxes. "But that is the last of my mother's gowns."

"I am sorry you had to do that." She touched the sleeve of his jacket. "Losing people you love is hard."

"I couldn't go through it again, loosing someone I love." He stepped even closer. "Patching a heart back together is not easy. Perhaps even impossible when it is already scarred."

Elizabeth looked up at him. He was so broad and towering he was all she could see—the stubble-peppered angles of his jawline, his straight nose, kissable lips, and intense gaze—yet she knew he had a vulnerable side to that strength.

"I hope you don't have to." She swallowed. Her pulse thudded in her ears. He was all she could focus on. "Do any patching, that is."

"So do I, Beth." He reached out and gently cupped her cheeks, his palms warm. "There was only you and I in Pheasant Lodge, and we were nothing but ourselves. I want that again." He came closer still, his chest almost touching hers.

"I believe we have spoken this evening with the same true tongues as we did upon our first meetings." Her voice was a breathy murmur.

"Aye, and I like it. What I don't like is when you don't believe my intentions. For they are only good, I only want to make you happy."

She wanted to be happy, she really did. And when she wasn't cross with Tom he did make her happy. She knew that. "I believe you are a good man, Tom. A very good man."

"That pleases me to hear." He lowered his face to hers, his lips a whisper away from kissing her.

"Tom?"

"My muse, my love, my Beth." He touched his lips to hers, not hard but not gentle—the kiss of a man who knew what he wanted.

A sense of relief came over her. Relief that she'd stopped fighting her body's desire. She opened her mouth and kissed him back. Stroking her tongue between his lips to find his.

Within a second, he'd embraced her fully and snapped her flush against his body. Taken control of the kiss entirely.

Her head spun, and she let out a groan of longing. The kiss deepened. He tasted of whisky and oak, and his breaths were coming fast, excited almost.

She looped her arms over his shoulders and raised her right leg, needing to be nearer to him.

He clutched her thigh, over her gown and pulled her knee higher, right up to his hip.

Their groins touched, through their clothing. His cock was hardening rapidly. The hardness of it, the thick wedge, thrilled her, and she squeezed nearer, running her hands into his hair.

"My beautiful Beth," he murmured. He kissed over her cheek and down her neck.

She tipped her head back and closed her eyes. She was in Pheasant Lodge again. Wanton. Lustful. Reckless. It was Tom who did this to her. Only Tom.

"Tom," she whispered, enjoying his name on her lips. "Oh, Tom."

He grasped her left buttock with his free hand. "I want to lie with you so badly."

"And I...so do I but..."

"There are no buts." He'd spoken onto her lips. "We are meant to be. Marry me."

"Tom...I..."

"I asked you before and you said no. You can see now, though, we are a perfect match, society will see that. Surely you can see that."

"I need to think about it. I—" He'd caught her mouth in another kiss, and all her thinking went out of the window.

He groaned as his cock pressed harder against her groin. The guttural, sexy sound sent a flurry of longing to her cunny. She ground against him, eliciting a riot of throbbing, hot sensations in her needy spot. If only the rest of the world could fade away again.

But that wasn't the case.

"Tom." She tore her mouth from his. "Please, we can't. We can't do this. Not now, not here."

"It's just a kiss." He released her leg and circled his arms around her waist.

"A kiss between two people who are not betrothed to one another."

He pulled in a deep breath and closed his eyes. "You are quite right. Plus we have both had rather our fill of whisky. We shouldn't let that cloud our judgment."

She studied him through narrowed eyes. It was true her head was a little fluffy and her limbs pliable, but she wasn't drunk, and neither was he. "You have changed your tune."

"I told you, Beth, I want to make you happy, and if this doesn't, if I don't—"

"I didn't say that."

"You didn't?"

"No." She untangled herself from him. "But I need to go. To my bedchamber. Sarah will wonder where I am."

"Of course. Let me show you the way."

She nodded and followed him from the quiet room. Once again he'd managed to persuade her to throw caution to the wind. Forget her place, her virtue. Yet all she could think about was that she'd lost his arms around her, his lips on hers, and the wonderful sensations being close to him brought to her body.

# Chapter Seventeen

Tom studied the temperamental sky. It wasn't ideal for a walk to Eagle Point, but he really wanted to show Beth his land. It was unique, rugged, beautiful, and he knew her keen artist's eye would appreciate it. He also hoped she'd fall in love with it, want to stay, want to make these hills her home.

"Please ensure Lady Burghley is warmly dressed," he said to Hamish. "Her lady's maid might not be as well versed on the inclement weather of the Highlands.

"Aye, your grace." Hamish helped Tom on with his heavy woollen greatcoat.

"And ensure Sarah is otherwise engaged when we leave for our walk."

"Your grace?"

"I do not wish for her to chaperone." Tom swiped up his gloves.

"I see. Of course. I am sure Cook will be able to find some jobs for her in the far kitchen garden."

"Excellent." Tom tugged on his hat. He was excited for the day.

"The sky was very red this morning." Hamish gestured to the bed-chamber window. "And the wind has changed to an easterly direction."

"Aye, I know. But we will risk it. The season is still kind in the majority, the sheep having only just gone to market."

"Very good."

The slightly lowered tone of Hamish's voice told Tom he wasn't fully approving of him going into the mountains. But was that because he was worried about the weather or the fact he was forgoing a chaperone? Tom didn't know, and he didn't much care. This was his land, his house, and he had every intention of making Elizabeth his wife before the year was out.

Hamish left the room, and Tom slipped a small paper bag of marzipan treats into his pocket along with a handkerchief embroidered with the Kilead crest.

He descended the stairs, the start of a new poem about late-night whisky and stolen kisses running through his mind.

After Tom had waited several minutes in the hallway, Beth appeared wearing stout leather boots, a thick shawl, mittens, and a woollen cap with a green bow on the front.

"Ah, excellent," he said. "The wind will not touch you up on the hillside."

"I hope not, for being cold isn't my favourite pastime." She smiled and glanced over her shoulder. "Where is Sarah?"

"I am not sure." He turned. "Hamish, where is Sarah?"

Hamish appeared, almost from the shadows. "I believe Cook has sent her on errands."

"Really?" Elizabeth said. "She was just with me."

"I expect Cook thought you had finished with her."

"No, I—"

"We do not need Sarah to accompany us," Tom said, taking her elbow. "We have had her company for two days of travelling."

"I know, but it is proper and—"

"You are not in England anymore, no longer watched over by the ton. At Kilead we can walk and talk as friends without having to be overseen."

She studied him. Her eyes narrow and one side of her mouth twitching.

"Come." He nodded at the door which Hamish had quickly opened. "There is much to see."

"You seem to want to invite a scandal."

"No, I am simply greedy and want you all to myself."

"Well, we shouldn't be too long," she said, "if we are unaccompanied."

"Whatever you wish." He steered her left. "This way."

To the left, the lawned garden etched with flower borders came to an end at a dry stonewall. Beyond that, the Highland moors stretched upwards, bruised with heather, dotted with small, dark-as-ink pools and lined with worn tracks.

A wooden stile made crossing the wall possible, and Tom offered his hand to Elizabeth. She held up her gown, revealing several layers of petticoats, and climbed over it.

"What do you think?" he asked when she stood on the moors for the first time.

With her hands on her hips, she nodded. "It's vast. It's all I can see for miles." She pointed at a towering peak in the distance. "Is that snow?"

"Aye, it's the first of the season, just a sprinkle, like Cook's sugar on mince pies."

"And the heather," she said, "it's so abundant."

"It likes the climate, but equally, the sheep do not like the heather."

She took a step onto the track. "Which way are we going?"

"Eagle Point is this way. It gets a wee bit steep at times, but I am sure you will manage well."

"Walking is the only way to get there?"

"A sure-footed horse would suffice, but I thought you might want to stop and study the nature under your boots."

"You are right."

They set off, the familiar track giving Tom a sense of peace. He was glad to be home. He was even more glad he had Beth with him.

After passing a stonewall in need of repair and walking alongside a babbling stream, they came to the last part of the climb.

Elizabeth was slightly out of breath, and her cheeks were pink.

"Do you need to rest?" he asked, concerned he was expecting too much from her.

"No, I am enjoying myself immensely. Your homeland is much more spectacular than I could have ever imagined. And I have seen not just heather and gorse but also thistle and bog myrtle, at least I think that's what they are."

Her words and enthusiasm thrilled him. "So next time you will bring your paints?"

"I will indeed." She continued on. Stomping over a dip in the track and around several large stones. To their left, a pair of red grouse squawked as they flew above the heather seeming to say 'go back, go back'.

Soon, they were at the top, a stunning elevation that gave a full circle of views over the entire Kilead estate.

"Perhaps we will see an eagle," Tom said, standing behind her and looking not at the view but at the way the strands of her hair peeking from her cap caught on the breeze.

"I would like that." She sighed and held her clenched hands beneath her chin. "It's all so beautiful."

Her shawl was deep purple, almost matching the heather when a cloud blocked the sun and darkened it. Her gown, a pale moss green, was dirtied a little around the base. Luckily, that didn't seem to bother her. Her attention was on the peaks and troughs of the Highlands, and he could almost feel her falling in love with it.

His arms ached to hold her, and he couldn't deny them, so he pressed up close behind her and pulled her to him, his arms circling her waist.

"Tom!"

She went to turn, but he stopped her and placed his mouth by her ear. "You are a painting rich with all colours. You are my never-ending story growing from a magical moment. You are that open, clear pool where no dark worries swim. You are my morn and sunset where warmth never fades." He closed his eyes, his heart feeling so full he feared it might burst. "Love is desire first held in the eye but quickly spreads to the heart. Know that without you I am but a bleeding heart cut with many biting blades. I am yours, captivated and enchanted, from this day until my last."

She was quiet.

He heard her swallow.

"It's just a rough draft of a poem that I've been working on," he said, inhaling her sweet flowery scent. "I still need to tweak it, make it flow better, and likely I've missed a few words out trying to remember it up here and—"

"It's beautiful." She rested her hands on his forearms and leaned back into him. "It really is, just as it is."

"I'm pleased you think so. My work has taken a different turn since I met you." He glanced at the sky. A silken grey weather front was creeping in from the east. "Being in love has inspired me more than I ever thought it would."

She stroked her hand over his coat, seeming to feel his forearm beneath. "Tom I—oh..." She drew in a sharp breath.

He knew why she'd gasped. A sudden hard stone had hit her, one had hit him, too, on the cheek, then another and another. Hailstones.

"Strewth." He looked upwards. How had he missed the marbled violet-grey cloud right above? He'd seen the darkening ones in the east but not the one stalking them.

"What will we do, Tom?" She spun around, clutching her cap against a gust of wind. Her eyes were wide, her shawl already speckled with tiny white balls of ice. "The weather, it has—"

"Quickly, this way." He clutched her hand and led her to the right, in the opposite direction of the way they'd come.

"No, we need to get back to the house."

"It's too far." He grimaced when the hail hit him full in the face, frozen little needles stabbing at him. "Beyond this bluff is a shepherd's cottage."

"But I..."

"Hurry." Cold blobs of rain were accompanying the hail now, and the wind had picked up to gale force, flapping his coat around his legs in a series of snaps. They'd be soaked through in minutes. He wrapped one arm around her waist, holding her to him as they rushed along. The last thing he wanted was for her ankle to turn on the stony path.

She was breathing hard to keep up with him, but when he glanced at her wet face he saw determination. Elizabeth was made of tough stock, he liked that. No tears, not protestations, just resolve to get out of the situation.

"It's not far," he called over the sudden whipping wind. "Just around this corner."

She nodded.

They negotiated a stream, hopping over the steppingstones to the opposite muddy bank. Her foot slipped, but he caught her, dragging her body to his.

"Are you hurt?"

"No. No. I'm fine." She nodded ahead. "Is that it?"

"Aye, I told you it wasn't far."

They rushed up to the small white cottage. It had one door, and two windows, one either side. The chimney stuck into the angry sky, smokeless, for the shepherd wasn't there.

"The sheep have been taken to market," he said. "But I will light a fire." He pushed into the dark interior of the cottage, the relief of being out of the hideous weather instantaneous. "Come in." He tugged her in with him. "And I'll..." He slammed the door.

The silence was almost as deafening as the sudden wind had been. His ears rang, and water dripped from his eyebrows, his nose and his chin. He looked at Elizabeth.

"My goodness." She pulled off her cap and blinked water from her eyelashes. "We were standing in sunshine and then..."

"It's very changeable in the mountains. But that was a particularly quick turnaround. Here, take this off, it's sodden." He removed her shawl and set it over the back of one of two chairs in the tiny kitchen area. "I'll light a fire and we can dry off before going back to Kilead."

"We definitely need to dry off."

"Aye, we do. It is the second time Mother Nature has sent us running indoors together to escape the weather."

"That is true." She paused. "Perhaps she is trying to tell us something. What that is, I don't know."

Tom did. They were meant to be. Destined.

Elizabeth sighed. "Oh dear." Her gloves were soaked, so was her gown from the waist down, the base not just a little dirty but splashed with globs of brown mud and speckled with dark, gritty earth. She frowned down at it. "What a state of affairs."

# Chapter Eighteen

"Do not worry," Tom said, taking off his coat and laying it over the back of the other chair. "I will soon have this little room warm, and tea for us to drink." He dug into his pocket. "Here, have some of these while I light the fire." He handed her a paper bag. "Marzipan."

"Thank you." She smiled and dug in for a sugary treat.

Tom strode to the fire and stooped, grabbed a handful of kindling.

Elizabeth noticed that his breeches were wet through, sticking to his flesh beneath, outlining the curve of his rear. His boots were mud-caked, and he'd left a trail across a faded red rug. The shepherd would likely be most unimpressed upon his return.

Within seconds, small flames were licking over the kindling. A piece of wood cracked, sending a spray of sparks.

Elizabeth shivered. Her petticoats were clinging to her legs like wet, gripping hands. Goose bumps danced on her flesh, the hairs on her arms rising. She wrapped her arms around herself and looked around.

Everything was in this one room, a bed stacked with blankets tucked into the corner. An area for food preparation along with several shelves of preserves, a milk urn, and stoneware containers. The wooden table was complete with a chipped plate, a stained cup, and two chairs. The fire and stove had a pot for heating food and a black kettle. Beside it, two soft chairs with fraying upholstery, a woodpile, a pair of old boots with a hole in the toe of one, and a length of string hanging from a nail in the whitewashed wall.

"Come here," Tom said, carefully stacking a log on the fire. "You'll catch your death."

She walked towards him, the heat from the flames beginning to grow now, but still she shivered.

"In the name of the Lord, you're dripping." He stood and frowned. "And this is all my fault."

"You're not in control of the weather, Tom." She nodded at his breeches. "And you are just as wet where your overcoat gave you no cover."

"I am not concerned about myself." His frown deepened. "Do not think I am being overly forward, but you must get out of those clothes before a chill sets in." He took her arm, prickled with goose bumps. "And it already is." He shook his head then strode to the bed. He grabbed a grey woollen blanket and shook it. "I beg you to wrap yourself in this while I dry your gown beside the fire."

"Tom, I..."

"It is not as if we are strangers." He held out the blanket and closed his eyes tight. "And I will not peep."

"But I—"

"Please. However will I forgive myself if you become sick because of my foolish desire to show you Eagle Point?"

"I wanted to see it." A full-body shiver attacked her, almost rattling her teeth. "But all right, I...I can't stay in these clothes."

Quickly, she began to strip off her gown, her petticoats and her boots and stockings. Everything was saturated; water dripped from her clothes and her hair. When she was naked, her nipples hard little pebbles, she walked into the blanket Tom was holding out.

He enclosed the warmth around her, his arms adding to it. Then rubbed her shoulders as if trying to keep her cold blood flowing.

"Better?" he asked.

"Yes."

"Good. Now sit beside the fire, warm yourself. I'll hang your clothes to dry and get water on to boil."

"Thank you." She sat on a soft chair.

Watching him move around, spreading her gown and petticoats on the length of string above the mantel, then filling the kettle, she couldn't help but be impressed at his ability to fix a situation. He might be a duke with many servants, but he could also look after himself, and her, so it seemed.

She gripped the blanket tighter, acutely aware of her nakedness beneath. Luckily, the shivering was slowing and the goose bumps receding.

He straightened and pushed his hand through his wet hair. Several drips flew into the air.

"Tom, you are still very wet," she said, worrying on her bottom lip.

"I will soon dry."

"But what if you catch your death?" She hesitated. "I would never forgive myself that it was showing me Eagle Point that led you to that state."

He glanced down at his breeches. "It is true, these are wholly unpleasant this wet."

"So hang them up." This time she bit on her bottom lip. Surely it was most sinful to suggest a man take off his clothes when they were alone together, no matter how wet they were.

For a moment he studied her, then he dragged off his boots and set them beside the fire next to hers. Then he walked to the bed, shook out a blanket, and wrapped it around himself. He set about taking off first his shirt and then his breeches. It was quite the jig to keep his modesty, and he was doing well until the last moment when the blanket fell and pooled at his feet.

Elizabeth's breath hitched. His perfect behind was pale, his legs long, and when he half turned to reach the blanket, she saw his cock for the second time.

"Darn it, I apologise," he said, folding the blanket around his waist. He walked to the fire, his jaw tight, and stood before it, hands outstretched and warming his palms.

She let her gaze slide down his body, making out the contours beneath the worn blanket. She wanted to know him better. The urge to touch him, experience flesh on flesh, was almost overwhelming. He was the most beautiful man she'd ever seen.

The words of his first draft poem came back to her.

*'Love is desire first held in the eye but quickly spreads to the heart. Know that without you I am but a bleeding heart cut with many biting blades. I am yours, captivated and enchanted, from this day until my last.'*

With a little jolt she realised they were true for her, too. Why was she denying that she was in love with Tom? She'd fallen for him in Pheasant Lodge, her heart had beat only for him ever since. He'd wanted to marry her from the start, and she had him. Her prayers had been heard, he wasn't a gamekeeper he was a man with a title, he could make her happy, she could make him happy. Society would highly approve of their union.

She shrugged the blanket from her shoulders and stood, leaving it on the chair. The cool air caressing her naked flesh was thrilling as she stepped up to him. "Tom," she said quietly.

He turned. His cheeks had pinked before the fire, and when he saw her nakedness, his eyes widened and his attention dipped to her breasts. "Beth, what are you doing?"

"Shh." She put her finger to his lips. "I want to tell you something."

"You do?" he managed.

"Yes." She slipped her finger over his chin, down his neck and to the hollow of his throat. She stared into his eyes and saw love and desire and kindness as well as a glint of anticipation. "I want to tell you that I will think very seriously about marrying you."

He swallowed, his Adam's apple bobbing. "You will?"

"Yes."

"When will you make a decision?"

"In two days."

He smiled. "So I have two days to win your heart."

"You already have my heart. I just need to learn a bit more about Kilead, life at Kilead. And you, life with you." She let her finger drift lower, to his sternum, and swirled her fingertip through his patch of body hair there. "I need to know if the Highlands are the right place for me to spend the rest of my life."

He pulled in a breath, his chest puffing up. "Beth," he murmured, his eyelids becoming a little heavy, as if he'd taken several whiskies. "I will make it right for you."

"Will you let me paint you?" she asked softly.

"You can do whatever the heck you want with me." He paused. "But, aye, of course you can paint me."

"I've perfected the art of capturing petals, leaves, and stems." She ran her finger to his right nipple. It was small and dark, and she circled it slowly. "And now I want to capture your body, every inch of it."

A tremble travelled over his skin. Was it a shiver, or was it her touch?

She hoped it was her touch.

He let out a long, low breath when she skimmed over his flesh to his other nipple. Hers were tingling, her heart racing. Touching him was so new and exciting and wrong—but heck, she didn't care that it was wrong. They'd be wed soon, she'd wager on it, and give themselves to each other with their bodies.

"You're teasing me the way the most mischievous of woodland nymphs might," he said breathlessly. "I ache for you all over. You have done that to me."

She held his gaze. "You truly ache for me?"

"Aye." His jaw tightened. "So much it is almost painful."

Ensuring her touch was slow and delicate, she dipped down to his navel, stroking his flesh, then lower still through the soft hair that led to his groin. Her journey stopped at the blanket fastened around his hips.

"Beth," he breathed.

The way he'd spoken her name had her back in Pheasant Lodge. A place where only they existed. Where the seeds of love had been planted.

"I want to feel how much you ache," she said then licked her lips, her mouth drying at the same time her cunny was dampening.

He parted his lips, but no words came out as she unhooked the blanket and let it fall to the floor.

His dark erection was thick and long, almost painful-looking it was so hard and swollen, and for a moment she stared at it.

He clenched his fists and sucked in a breath. Closed his eyes. There seemed to be a great harness of willpower and self-control.

"Tom," she said and rested one hand on his shoulder. "Look at me."

He did what she'd asked, and when she had his attention fixed on her, she took his warm cock in her hand and held it firm.

"Merciful heavens," he gasped. "What are you doing?"

"I want to touch you, feel your pleasure the way you've felt mine."

"I thought we were never to talk of that." His voice was strained.

"I've changed my mind, for today, here, we are back in Pheasant Lodge, nothing but a gamekeeper and a village girl." She ran her hand up to the tip of his cock then down to the root where it sprang from his body. "No one to disturb us."

"Your hand on me..." He wrapped one arm around her waist and set his other palm over her right breast. "Is what I have dreamed of."

"You are not dreaming now." His touch had her flesh tingling again, not with cold this time but with desire.

He let out a low groan. She continued to work him up and then down his cock.

"Am I doing it right?" she asked, reaching up to speak against his lips.

He groaned again. "Can't you tell?"

"You're the first man I've touched," she said.

"Which makes this all the more enchanting." He released her breast and wrapped his big hand over hers. "A bit faster, like this." He set the pace, moving her hand.

His cock grew even harder. A slick of moisture seeped from the end onto her thumb, and she used it as lubrication.

"Ah, yeah." He released her hand and slotted his fingers into her hair, pulled her close for a kiss.

It was a fast, hard kiss, breathless, too. She had a sense of power, of holding him, owning him.

"Don't stop," he gasped. He broke the kiss and stared into her eyes. "I beg you, don't stop."

"I won't. Not until you tell me to."

He clenched his jaw, his teeth gritting. His nostrils flared, and a glaze crossed his eyes.

Excitement winged through Elizabeth. He'd seen her take pleasure, felt her pleasure, and now she was going to experience his. He was a storm about to unleash, a wild stallion about to break free.

"That's it. Aye. Oh..." He caught her mouth, his tongue searching for hers. His cock pulsed, sending his seed bursting free and coating her hand.

She didn't let up, gripping him tight, her hand sliding on his length up and down, over and over.

Another burst of fluid accompanied by a long, guttural groan. He threw his head back, face to the ceiling, neck tendons straining. "In the Devil's name...heaven help me."

"Tom," she said, worrying he was in pain. Had she done it wrong at the last moment?

"Oh..." He shuddered. "My Beth, I do declare that was the most intense..." He was breathing hard. "Amazing thing I have ever felt."

"I did it right?"

He captured her hand and stopped her working him. "More than right. Perfect."

"Good, because I wanted to please you."

"And now I want to please you."

"I...oh...!"

He'd dragged her close, then backed her up to the wall that ran beside the fire.

"Like this," he said. In one swift move, he captured her wrists and hauled her arms above her head.

The wall was cool on the bare skin of her shoulders and buttocks, and she arched her back against it. A thrill went through her when she saw the determined glint in his eyes.

"I am not the type of man who will take pleasure without giving it in return," he said hotly against her lips. "So get ready to be crying out my name in ecstasy within the next few minutes."

# Chapter Nineteen

Tom stared down at the beautiful woman trapped and at his mercy. Her pupils were wide, her cheeks flushed, and her hard nipples poked against his chest.

His cock had been satisfied, but his honour had not. For what honourable man didn't ensure his woman also climaxed?

"Tom," she gasped, squirming but going nowhere.

He held her firm.

"You are so beautiful," he said. He slid his free hand down her throat to her left breast. He cupped its weight in his hand and stroked his thumb over the taut little nipple.

She hauled in a breath, her chest rising upwards.

"Tell me you want me to touch you," he said hoarsely. "Tell me what you want."

"Oh, Tom. We shouldn't, and I..."

"Forget the rules. The rule book has been torn up." He gritted his teeth and squeezed up against her. "Tell me what you want, deep down, in the very core of your soul."

"I want you to..."

"Do you want me to do this?" He slipped his hand lower, over her soft belly to the hair at the juncture of her thighs. "You want me to touch your cunny? Your special erotic place?"

"Yes." She parted her legs and canted her hips forward. "Oh yes. Please."

He smiled then kissed her, his lips still curled at the edges. And as his tongue probed her mouth, his finger probed her velvety entrance. She was hot and wet and her arousal slick. When he pushed to his knuckle, she groaned and dropped her weight onto the invasion.

But he kept her trapped, her torso stretched, her arms pinned. If she was seriously thinking about marrying him, he wanted her to know he could give her everything she needed, in every aspect of her life.

"You feel amazing," he said, their noses touching. "And if we marry, know this. My cock will ride into your cunny, and when I fill you with seed, you will find the most exquisite pleasure of all. We will cry out each other's names. Cling to each other. Never want to leave the bedchamber." He flicked his thumb over her nub.

She groaned, her knees seeming to give way. "More."

"I can give you more." He added another finger then set his thumb to work. "I'll give you more every day and every night. You will be intoxicated with pleasure, drunk on my love. I will ensure you are the most satisfied, worshipped wife who has ever walked this earth."

Her eyes fluttered shut, and her lips parted.

He upped the tempo, using his fingers the way he would like to use his cock. Penetrating deep and fast. Urging her nearer to climax.

"Ah... I don't know if...I can stand up for this." She trembled and balled her hands into fists.

"I've got you," he said. "I will always hold you up."

She whimpered. A soft little mewling sound that had blood rushing to his cock again.

Her body was soft and pliant but at the same time rigid, a spring about to uncoil.

His palm was wet now, her moisture leaking from her with each thrust of his fingers. "Show me your pleasure, take it," he whispered onto her lips. "I won't let you fall."

She stared into his eyes, but he wasn't sure how much she was seeing. Ecstasy had stolen her, taken her breath, too.

Suddenly, she dropped into his hold entirely. Lost to her release. "Tom. Tom...oh...Lord above..."

She climaxed. Her cunny gripped his fingers over and over, more fluid leaking onto his hand. He kept on giving her pleasure, committing every moment to memory. She was incredible. The most responsive and sweet woman he'd ever known.

"Oh please...oh...no more." She wriggled. "I..."

"I've got you," he said again and withdrew. "I've got you, I promise." He released her wrists and dragged her naked body close to his. He tucked her head beneath his chin. Her breasts were warm and soft and her breaths fast and hot on his neck.

She clung to his shoulders, her little fingers digging in tight.

"When we lie together it will be even better," he whispered. "We will find our pleasure at the same time and swirl together in bliss."

She didn't reply, just sagged closer and let out a small moan.

So he stooped, picked her up, and walked to the soft chair she'd been sitting in. Sitting with her on his lap, he wrapped her discarded blanket around them both and held her tight. Their bodies fit together as though made for each other.

While she caught her breath, he watched the flames dancing. Surely she would accept his marriage proposal. How could she not? They were so in tune. He'd never want another woman other than her.

If she said no, he'd commit to a life of bachelorhood, likely celibacy, too, for what would be the point of being with another woman and thinking only of Beth?

The hailstones set up another round of sharp assault, tapping angrily against the windows, door, and roof. A few made their way down the chimney and sizzled into the fire or rolled onto the rug only to quickly melt.

"Are you warm enough?" he asked, kissing the top of her head.

"Yes. And full of shame. We shouldn't have done that."

"Shh." He frowned. "God blessed us with desire, so surely it would be more shameful not to act upon it?"

She studied him for a few moments, then, "I think you should put that point of view into your poetry and see how well it is received by the masses."

"You do?"

She laughed and sat up straighter. "If you think your pen name will protect you from the zealots."

He chuckled. "I'm not sure it would."

"I have to get up and see if my gown is dry."

"It isn't." He held her closer. There was no way he was going to let her sweet body leave his just yet. Her soft rear on his thighs and her breasts within reach had his cock in a semi-hard state, and he was thoroughly enjoying it. "Stay here, for a few moments longer. We are utterly alone."

"Will Hamish search for us?" Panic crossed her features.

"No, he knows full well I am capable of taking care of myself in the Highlands."

"Are you sure?"

"I am." He tilted her chin and kissed her. If he had his way, they'd stay in the shepherd's cottage forever. Live simply and easily with the mountains and the seasons. But Beth deserved more. She deserved gowns made of the finest silk. Meals created by expert cooks. Fine wine. Finer whisky. And a warm, plush home to raise their children.

Children.

Oh aye. He wanted Beth to carry his children. She was the only woman he could imagine giving birth to his heir.

And all she had to do was say yes.

Yes to marrying him. One little word.

And his life would be complete, and he'd make damn sure hers was, too.

Sometime later, Tom stood to tend the fire. When he'd done that, naked, he turned and spotted Beth slipping on her silken petticoats which had dried quickly.

"I prefer you without clothes," he said, twitching his eyebrows.

"That does not surprise me."

She touched her hair. It had lost several pins. Her breasts rose then jiggled slightly as she adjusted it, and he had to stop himself for reaching out for her, dipping his head and taking her tempting nipples into his mouth.

"We should make our way back, before the sky darkens again." She nodded at the window.

Tom grabbed his breeches, which were now only a little damp, and pushed aside the flimsy curtain. "The weather might hold, for a while at least. So aye, let's get back to Kilead, hunger will soon set in."

It was not pleasant putting on damp clothes, but at least they weren't sopping.

Soon, they were heading back over the stream and the stepping-stones, past Eagle Point and then making their way along the heather-lined track.

"Over there." Tom suddenly stopped and pointed to the right. "Can you see?"

"What is it?" She also came to a halt.

"A rut. Two stags, just beyond that tree." He stood beside her, head close, and directed her line of sight.

"I can't see anything."

"Aye, you can. Look closer, they're the colour of hazelnuts."

The sound of antlers colliding clacked through the air.

"Yes, I see them," she said. "Gosh, aren't they magnificent."

"The best stock around for miles."

For a few moments, they watched in silence. She appeared as in awe as he was.

"Will they come this way?" she asked when one turned and stared in their direction.

"Hopefully not, because they're clearly in foul moods." He slid his arm around her waist. "Let's not push our luck."

They carried on their way. The wind was cold, chilling his breeches to his legs and poking through every nook and cranny of his coat to nip at his skin.

He was worried about Beth; she, too, was cold. And her face was pale. The wind seeming to have blown the colour from her cheeks.

With their breath clouding before their faces, finally, they made their way onto the front drive of Kilead. The rain was coming again, big fat drips that plopped onto the ground.

Hamish was pacing on the steps, the door open behind him. "Your grace, you are both wet to the skin."

"We are not that bad, but certainly cold." Tom ushered Beth inside. The sooner she was out of the elements the better.

"The heavens opened." Hamish closed the huge heavy door. "I prayed you'd taken shelter."

"We did. In the shepherd's cottage."

"Aye, that's good."

"Can you send for Lady Burghley's maid at once. She needs to bathe and warm up."

"Certainly. And I shall organise tea and bone broth."

"Thank you." He turned to Beth. "I will help you to your room. I fear you will catch a chill if we do not take immediate action."

She sneezed, her hands coming to her face. "Excuse me."

"Bless you." Damn it. Were they too late? He sent a quick prayer to God as they climbed the stairs.

Sarah was already in Beth's bedchamber, her fingers knotted and a fire raging. "Oh, I have been so worried. I should have been with you, I am so sorry, I—"

"No apologies." Beth held up her hand. "And it is for the best, otherwise we would both be in a chilled state and of no use to each other."

"Yes, of course, my lady. Hot water is filling the tub this very moment, I've kept it over the kitchen fire in anticipation of you returning with your clothes dripping with Highland rain." She looked at Tom. "If you could excuse us, I really must get my mistress out of this gown before she gets ill." She shook her head and frowned. "Indeed, you already resemble undercooked pastry."

# Chapter Twenty

Elizabeth shivered and placed the soles of her feet on the freshly heated foot warmer Sarah had just slid beneath the blankets. Her skin tingled, but not in a pleasant way, in an itchy, crawling ants way. And her temples throbbed as though someone with giant hands was squeezing her head.

"Oh dear, this is what I feared." Sarah touched Elizabeth's brow.

"What?"

"You have a fever."

"I'm sure I don't." She swallowed, her throat scratching the way it would if she tried to eat nettles. She grimaced.

"You do, my lady." Sarah squeezed out a flannel and placed it on her head.

It was cool and sent a new shiver over Elizabeth's scalp and down her spine.

"I will have to tell His Grace."

"Please, don't bother him."

"He will be angered if I don't." She paused. "He cares for you very much, that is clear to see."

Elizabeth was quiet.

Sarah poured her a lemon and honey tea.

"Thank you." She took it, the sweet citrus scent wafting up her nose. "How are you finding Kilead, Sarah?"

"I like it."

"You do? It is so different to Burghley."

"Yes, it is, but the views are beautiful. The mountains, the lochs, the eagles soaring overhead. And even the wild weather, it is quite thrilling, don't you think?"

"Not when caught in it." Elizabeth sipped her tea.

"Of course not. Forgive me."

"And the staff? Are they friendly?"

"Oh, ever so friendly, my lady. Cook is not at all short-tempered with me, even though I don't know where anything is when she asks me to help her. And Hamish has been so kind. He's such a gentleman, even with that big carrot-coloured beard of his and his hands the size of dinner plates. And Colm..."

"Colm?"

"Yes, one of the footmen, he's..."

"What?" Elizabeth studied Sarah curiously. "What is he?"

Sarah shrugged and turned away, but Elizabeth saw the coy smile balling her cheeks.

"He's kind, too..." Sarah said, "and funny and handsome."

"He is?"

"Yes, he's got dimples." Sarah giggled. She poked her fingers onto her cheeks. "Right here, both sides, and when he laughs you can see them."

"How old is he?"

"He is two years older than me." She gave a shrug, her eyes taking on a distant glaze. "He is unmarried."

"Ah, I see." Elizabeth had never seen Sarah this way. "So it would suit you to stay here a little while longer?"

"Yes, my lady. I am happy here." She paused. "As long as you are, that is."

"I like it." Elizabeth sipped her tea then nibbled on her bottom lip. It was time to speak to one of the few people she could absolutely trust. "The duke has asked me to marry him."

"He has?" Sarah's eyes widened. "Oh, my lady, that is wonderful news..." She rushed up to the bed, her hands clasped beneath her chin. "Isn't it?"

"Yes, I think so."

"You think so?" She frowned.

Elizabeth held her breath. Her nose was tickling. It was no good. She sneezed. The flannel on her brow flew off and landed wetly on the blanket.

"My lady, this is a terrible chill you have caught." Sarah grabbed the flannel and resoaked it. She carefully laid it back on Elizabeth's forehead.

"I am sure I will survive." Elizabeth sighed. "God willing."

"God willing indeed." Sarah paused. "And what did you say? When His Grace asked you?"

"I told him I'd consider it."

"You are a very good match and make a very handsome couple." Sarah nodded. "I am sure Lord and Lady Burghley would approve wholeheartedly."

"I don't disagree, they would be very happy. But it would mean a move, a permanent move, here, to Kilead. It is a long way from home."

Sarah dipped her head. "You must do what you think is right for you, my lady. What your heart is telling you to do."

"I am trying to listen to my heart." Elizabeth finished her tea then passed the cup to Sarah.

Sarah set the cup aside.

"But it's very hard to think when I feel so rotten." Elizabeth shivered. Despite the layers of blankets, the foot warmer, and the fire, she was still cold.

"I beg you not to give it another thought until you are better." Sarah tucked the blankets around Elizabeth's feet. "You need to rest. And the more rest the better. I will go and ask Cook to make some liquorice lozenges, right this instant, and later you can suck on them to restore your strength."

"Good idea." Elizabeth closed her eyes, suddenly feeling weary and somewhat dizzy. "I will sleep now."

For a few minutes, Sarah fussed with the curtains and the fire, then the quiet click of the door signified Elizabeth was alone.

Quickly, her thoughts fractured, and sleep stole her away. But it wasn't a restful sleep, her dreams were full of spiders and snakes, black shadows creeping around her, and heavy, hot bricks raining down from the sky.

She awoke sweating and gasping for breath, flung the blankets off, and reached for a glass of water.

"Here, let me."

Tom was at her side, holding the water. His brow was creased in a frown, and the buttons on his white shirt were undone.

"Thank you," she croaked.

He set the glass at her lips, and she sipped.

"You have been battling nightmares," he said, shaking his head. "Terrible nightmares."

"Yes. I am glad to wake up." The fire had turned to embers. The curtains were fully closed now, indicating darkness had fallen. She'd slept longer than she'd thought.

"Do you have a fever?" Tom stood and touched her brow. "Mmm..."

"I am hot, but perhaps just too many blankets. It is not winter yet."

"This is true."

Suddenly, her stomach gurgled. "Oh, pardon me."

"You need to eat." He walked to the call bell and rang it. "It will do you the world of good. Cook has fixed bubble and squeak, and it is the best. It always saw me right as rain when I was a wee lad and got into a fix."

"Thank you."

"And I will call for the doctor."

"The doctor?"

"Aye."

"No, please don't, Tom. I am not that sick, and surely he must have a long way to travel in bad weather and the dark."

"That is not our concern if he is required."

"Please, don't send for him, I am hardly at death's door. Some rest and food and—" She pushed herself to sitting then flopped back on the pillows.

"I insist." He placed his hands on his hips.

"And I insist you don't." She paused. Her throat really was horribly sore. "I am not some damsel in distress. I will be well by morning with rest and bubble and squeak."

His lips twisted as if he was thinking hard.

"If I am still feverish and sick then, you may call him."

He sighed. "I will tolerate that, but only because you are well enough to argue your case."

"Thank you." She sighed. "Could you call for some honey and lemon tea, please, I rather enjoyed it a little while ago."

"That was over eight hours ago, it is well past midnight now."

"What? Cook shouldn't be worrying about preparing me food, and Tom, you should be in bed." She frowned. "Really, it's not proper for you to be in my room at all."

He raised his eyebrows. "We are past being proper, don't you agree?"

"Do not speak like that. We shouldn't, we've been—"

"What's happened has happened, and I don't regret any of it for a single moment. And you should understand that I could not sleep knowing you had a fever." He sat on the bed and took her hand. "I am not only racked with guilt but also filled with fear."

"Guilt? But why?"

"It was my insistence we walk to Eagle Point that has made you this way and—"

"I already told you, I wanted to go, and no one could have predicted the weather changing. It was sunny when we left."

He frowned as though her words irritated him more.

"And why are you fearful?"

"You know why." He drew her hand to his lips and gently kissed the back of her knuckles.

"Tell me."

"I cannot bear the thought of losing you. If a fever stole you away, how would I breathe? How could my heart beat? I would become a shadow of a man, Beth. I can't imagine my life without you."

"Oh, Tom. Do not fear, you will not have to live without me. I am made of strong blood. A day in bed, and I will be as good as new."

"I hope that is the case, but..."

"But?"

"But I hope this has not put you off Kilead...off me. I would hate the hailstorm to be a black mark against our marrying."

With her free hand she touched his cheek. "Do you really think the power of a storm is anything compared to the power of love?" She paused and looked into his eyes—kind, passionate, intelligent eyes that she'd come to adore. "It isn't. And I do love you, Tom, very much."

"You do?"

"Yes, I have from the beginning, from when we were at Pheasant Lodge, and now..."

He appeared to hold his breath, waiting for her next words.

"But I just need a little more time. And my head...it's foggy." She touched her brow. "This chill has made me somewhat hazy in my thoughts."

He released his breath. "I understand. Of course I do."

*Knock. Knock.*

"Enter," Tom called.

Sarah stepped in carrying a small tray holding a bowl with a plate over the top. "Oh, your grace, I wasn't expecting you to be in here." She dipped her head.

"I heard Lady Burghley having a nightmare. I was concerned." His jaw tightened. That was the end of the matter.

"Oh dear, another one." Sarah rushed over to the bed and set the tray on a round table. "This is really not good. You are quite delirious, my lady."

"It is true I am sick, but I'm sure I will be well soon."

"We have struck a deal to call the doctor in the morning if no improvement," Tom said.

"Perhaps we should send for him now?" Sarah fussed with Elizabeth's pillows.

"No, no." Elizabeth nodded at the bowl. "That smells delicious. I have an appetite, which must be a good sign."

"Yes. It is." Sarah carefully passed her the tray. She turned to Tom. "I will sit with Lady Burghley until morning if you want to get some rest, your grace."

Tom studied Sarah, seeming to decide whether or not he could trust her.

"I will be in good hands. Sarah has been at my side for a long time through good and bad times," Elizabeth said. "Really, you should rest or you will also get sick."

He kind of huffed and stood. "I will rest, then tomorrow, if you are feeling up to it, I will read to you."

"That would be lovely. Thank you." She smiled at him. "Sleep well."

Elizabeth slept until the sun had reached its highest point. And when she awoke she was refreshed, her skin had stopped prickling, and her head was clearer. There was no denying the barbing scratch in her throat, but that was soothed with warm honey and lemon tea, and she kept a bowl of liquorice lozenges close.

Sarah helped her wash and change her nightgown. She also brought fresh pillows and blankets and a slice of fruitcake.

"You must be tired," Elizabeth said, frowning at several strands of Sarah's hair that had escaped her tight bun. "You have been up most of the night, you poor thing."

"I am here to do your bidding, my lady."

"And you have fulfilled your duty, I feel much better." She paused and glanced at the screen that covered the door to Tom's room. "Perhaps you could ask His Grace if he would come and read to me now. I'm sure when he sees me he'll realise there is no need to call a doctor."

"Of course. I will let him know." She bobbed her head and disappeared.

Elizabeth sighed, and her gaze was taken to the large window. The view was incredible. Giant mountains set against a sky heavy with bulbous white clouds that were skittering east as though in a rush to get to some place. The mountains weren't forested, they were thick with heather and gorse, smudges of lilac, purple, and pink, reminding her of paint on paper, dashed on using a thick brush.

A dense murmuration of starlings danced in the distance, silhouetted against the clouds.

She thought of the stags rutting and wondered where they'd travelled to today. Tom's land was vast. Everything they'd seen, even in the far distance on their walk, had belonged to him.

"Ah, you're awake and with a wee bit of colour in your cheeks." Tom strode towards her, having used their connection door.

She smiled. "Yes. I am well rested and feeling much better."

"So no need for the doctor, or would you still like me to fetch him to check you over?"

"That won't be necessary. I have eaten and washed. Nothing to remark on other than a slightly sore throat."

"Mmm."

"That does not require medical attention." She set her lips in a firm line.

He chuckled. "Okay, my lady. No doctor."

"You said you'd read to me."

"And I will." He held up a book, the cover decorated with trees. "This was my mother's."

"What is it?"

"*Romance of the Forest* by Ann Radcliffe. Have you heard of it?"

"Yes, and I wanted to read it."

"Good, then if you are comfortable, we shall begin."

Elizabeth settled back and closed her eyes. Tom's deep voice filled the room. He read eloquently and soon brought Monsieur Pierre de la Motte and Madame Constance de la Motte to life from the pages.

After a few chapters he stopped. "You should have some tea."

"I would like that. Will you take some, too?"

"Aye. I'll call for some, and perhaps some apricot ice-cream?"

"I am certainly being well fed here at Kilead."

"As is only right." He stood, set the book aside, and rang the bell.

Hamish appeared in moments.

When they were alone again, Elizabeth studied him. Like when he'd sat with her in the night he wore a white shirt with pale breeches, the top two buttons on the shirt undone, revealing some of his chest, almost down to where the sprinkle of hair at his sternum began. The sleeves were rolled up, his tendon-rich forearms on show. And his hair was a little unkempt, the way she'd seen him many times at Pheasant Lodge. She liked this look. It was a far cry from his formal attire when he'd surprised her at the ball. This was her Tom. Relaxed, at ease, being himself, doing things he enjoyed. "Can I ask you something?"

"Anything." He sat and folded his arms. The sun streaming through the window caressed his hair with gold and cast one side of his face in shadow.

"Can I paint you?"

His eyes widened slightly. "Paint me?"

"I told you before I wanted to."

"Aye, you did." He smiled. "Am I to become your muse the way you are mine?"

"Do you want to be?"

"I would be honoured." He chuckled.

With a smile, she gestured to the drawer containing her paper and paints. "As I have been ordered by both yourself and Sarah to remain in bed, could you please pass my paints and brushes."

"You want to do it now?"

"Yes. What else have I to do? And besides, the lighting is exquisite."

"I suppose you are right, there is little else for you to do." He gathered her equipment.

"Thank you. Now sit there again, the way you were."

He did as she'd asked, back rod-straight, chin tilted, lips a tight line. He gripped the arms of the chair.

She laughed. "This is not a formal portrait, relax."

"I am relaxed."

"I am inclined to disagree." She pointed to the book. "Why don't you keep reading while I paint?"

"You will still be able to paint me?"

"I'm new to painting the human form, but I think so." She hovered her brush, loaded with the palest brown on the tip, over the paper. "At least I'll try."

"Just don't make me look like an ogre." He picked up the book and flicked it open.

"I won't." She studied him. "Can I ask you to do one more thing?"

"Of course."

"Just...here..." She touched her sternum. "Can you...?"

"What?"

"Undo your shirt a bit more."

One side of his mouth tilted into a grin. "Are you meaning for this to be an erotic painting?"

"No, no, not at all." She giggled, a burst of energy. "It's just I like Gamekeeper Tom, you weren't wearing a shirt the first time I saw you."

"Ah, I see." He undid his shirt the final two buttons so that it showed the hair at his chest. "How is that?"

"Better, thank you." She liked the hollow of his throat, the shadows there that tapered downwards. "You can start reading now, and I'll start painting."

He did as she'd asked.

Soon, she was lost to the sound of his voice again and to the dabs of her brush. The colours were vivid and rich, dramatic almost, despite the calmness of the room. His features took shape, his heavy brows, straight nose, angular jawline, and she paid extra special attention to his eyes, even though his lids were lowered as he read. She wanted to capture the determination she saw there, plus his kindness.

The linen on his shirt was a little creased, and she added that in, as well as the fact his left sleeve was rolled higher than the right. And as she came to finishing the piece, the sun just slipping towards a jagged bluff, she decided she really was quite pleased with her first attempt at human form.

"Tom! Tom! Thomas Kilead, where on earth are you?" A high-pitched female voice. A bang. A door slam. "Bossy big brother of mine. Where are you?"

Tom snapped the book closed. "Gwen. She's back."

"Where you expecting her?"

"Well, aye, you know I was."

He turned to the screen, and at that moment, a young woman in a bright-yellow dress rushed from behind it carrying a small brown paper parcel.

When she saw them, she stopped in her tracks. "Oh! I say." She let the parcel hang at her side. "You must be Lady Elizabeth Burghley."

"Yes." Elizabeth tensed. It really was quite improper to be caught alone like this with Tom, in her bed, wearing nightwear, and Tom with his shirt undone, reading to her. It was almost as if they were a married couple already.

"Hamish said you were sick. How are you feeling now?" She sauntered up to the bed, her eyes glistening and a tiny smile tickling her lips.

"Much better, thank you."

"Gwen." Tom set the book aside and stood. "You appear in rude health. Edinburgh suits you."

"Ah yes." She turned her head so her brother could kiss her cheeks. "It is always a rush of dances, shopping trips, and afternoon tea. Auntie took me to the opera which was simply wonderful. And I absolutely must go back at the start of the winter season. The Lamonts are holding their most lavish ball ever, and Auntie thinks I should be one of the debutantes. Really, you should come, brother, there will be many eligible ladies there. You might finally bag yourself a wife." She rolled her eyes, and then her attention settled on Elizabeth's painting. "Oh, what are you doing?"

In an instant, she'd snatched the pad up and was holding it at arm's length, examining the portrait. "Well, I never did." She shook her head. "This is quite the painting of the Duke of Farrington. He almost looks human." She laughed.

"Gwen." Tom tried to take it, but she whirled away. "That's Beth's. I mean, Lady Burghley's."

"And was *Beth* not planning on showing it to you?"

"Well, I..." Tom frowned. "I suppose so when it's finished."

"It is finished." Elizabeth smiled at him. "See what you think."

Gwen was grinning broadly as she handed it to her brother.

Tom didn't speak. He just stared at it. A slight crease formed between his eyebrows.

Elizabeth swallowed, her throat scratching. What if he hated it? What if he told her to stick to flowers?

"It's brilliant, don't you think." Gwen clapped and hopped on the spot. "Such a good likeness, and with this..." She flapped her hand at Tom's undone buttons. "Well, it's almost...saucy."

"Saucy!" Elizabeth said. "That wasn't my intention, I was simply painting what I saw."

"Well, I think you saw Tom in a way not many people do." Gwen put her right hand on her hip. "And I, for one, like it."

"So do I." Tom dragged his attention from the painting to Elizabeth. "Very much." He smiled, a lovely warm smile that changed his face from being austere to gentle.

"Are you sure?"

"Aye. You are a truly talented artist."

"Isn't she just!" Gwen grinned and looked from her brother to Elizabeth. "We should all dine together this evening. I simply must learn more about our houseguest. I am totally intrigued."

Elizabeth laughed. "There is not much to know."

"Ah, but there is. Anyone who can make my brother smile like that..." She pointed at Tom. "Is someone I want to know."

"Gwen," Tom said. "Beth...Lady Burghley is recovering—"

"Oh, just call her Beth in front of me, it's clear that is what you call her when you're alone." Gwen flapped her hand. "And I know she is recovering from a chill and on bed rest, Hamish told me. So we will dine in here tonight. I will have the table set in the window, you can't possibly disagree with that."

"I would love to hear all about your time in Edinburgh," Elizabeth said. "It is a place I'd love to visit."

"Oh, and you will." Gwen plonked down on the bed, still holding her parcel. "You shall come with me. I will show you the best places. And Auntie, she will adore you. Oh, and there are rumours of a festival coming to the streets. Entertainers of all kinds. It will be the most incredible fun." She gestured to Tom. "I nearly forgot, I got you a book." She handed him the parcel.

"You did? Thank you." He opened it. "*Frankenstein* by Mary Shelley."

"Have you read it?"

"No, I haven't even heard of it."

"That is because you never go to the ton." She rolled her eyes. "Rumour has it, Mary Shelley had somewhat a competition with Lord Byron."

"The poet?"

"The very one." Gwen's eyes sparkled. "They had a competition to see who could write the best horror story. Mary Shelley came up with this, a story about a scientist who tried to create a person, or life, but instead created a monster. I think you will like it, brother."

"Why thank you for thinking of me and monsters at the same time." He studied the cover of the book. "What did Lord Byron write? Who won the competition?"

"I believe his story has not yet been published. But be safe in the knowledge I will source it for you when it does come to the bookshops. I know how you admire Byron."

# Chapter Twenty-One

The evening meal was an unusual affair. Not that Elizabeth hadn't dined in a bedchamber before, she had, but to have company and be seated in bed was most different.

The fire had been stoked, the curtains drawn and numerous candles lit. Cook had excelled with a chicken stew, herb dumplings, and fresh bread. They ate brandy snaps stuffed with apricot ice-cream for dessert.

Gwen was a bubbling cauldron of chatter and excitement, full of tales of Edinburgh and the people there. Her enthusiasm made Elizabeth long to visit. She flitted from one subject to another like a butterfly. Commenting on fashion and food, and new plays and books. It was no wonder she was the last to finish her food.

When Hamish and Colm had cleared away the plates—Colm a tall, pleasant young man with fair skin and freckles—Tom ordered three glasses of whisky.

"You know something," Gwen said when she had her drink in hand. "This has been a most pleasant return to Kilead. I am so pleased you are here, Lady Burghley."

"Please, call me Elizabeth."

"Elizabeth? Not Beth?"

"Only my father calls me Beth and—"

"And my brother." Gwen grinned and sipped her whisky.

"Yes, and your brother."

"I misheard her name when I first made her acquaintance," Tom said. "And it stuck."

"And where was this acquaintance made? Some fabulous ball at dear Gerald's, I'm guessing?"

Elizabeth glanced at Tom. He held her gaze for a second, then, "Not quite."

"So how?" Gwen's eyes sparkled, and she leaned forward, clearly eager for information.

"Let's just say as two creative souls we were drawn to one another." Tom tilted his chin and clamped his lips shut.

"I know there is a story behind this. A story you are not telling me." Gwen laughed; it was almost a cackle. "But that's all right, I am a patient woman and I'm positive one of you will tell me, some day."

"I wouldn't be so sure." Tom's jaw tightened.

"Oh, in the name of the Lord, now I am even more intrigued." Gwen finished her whisky in one mouthful. "And I am also exhausted. I am going to turn in. I bid you good night."

"And you, it's been lovely to spend time with you, Gwen." Elizabeth smiled at her. "I hope we will have many more nice evenings together."

"So do I." She looked at her brother. "Because you have done something to my brother no one has before."

"Gwen." Tom frowned.

But Gwen carried on. "He's had so much responsibility from such a young age. And I include myself in that. Sometimes I worried he'd forgotten how to smile. But here, now, with you, Elizabeth, it seems he can't stop smiling. And for that I am truly grateful." She pushed her hair over her shoulders. "Perhaps you won't need to come to the winter season balls in Edinburgh, Tom, in order to find a wife. Perhaps you will be wed by then. You should ask this fine woman, you'd be perfect together, only a fool would disagree."

Tom stood. "Gwen, don't speak out of line."

"You know I speak only the truth." She blew a kiss at Elizabeth and then Tom. "Sleep tight. Don't let the bed bugs bite."

She slipped from the bedchamber, a giggle seeming to follow in her wake.

"I am truly sorry. She has few faults, but talking non-stop and not stopping talking when it comes to matters that don't concern her are her weaknesses."

"Please, don't apologise." Elizabeth set her glass on the bedside cabinet. "I think she's wonderful. You should take full credit for raising an intelligent, confident, beautiful young woman. It's plain to see she has a good heart."

"She has." Tom sighed and sat on the bed. He took her hand and rubbed the pad of his thumb over her knuckles.

"Tom."

"Yes."

"In Pheasant Lodge when I said I couldn't marry you and that was something that would sadden me eternally, I meant it."

He was quiet, waiting for her to go on.

"And now, I've thought about it, a lot. And I don't have to be saddened eternally for not being able to marry you, do I?"

"No, you don't."

She smiled. "I still love you, Tom, even more than on that day at Pheasant Lodge when I was so bereft at our parting, so in answer to your question—"

"Go on..." His grip on her hand tightened.

"I will marry you. I will make Kilead my home. And I will do my best to provide you with an heir and be a dutiful wife."

He smiled broadly, the corners of his eyes creasing. "My beautiful Beth." He scooted closer and cupped her cheeks. "You have just made me the happiest man in Scotland, heck, in all the world, and if I wasn't concerned for your health, I would ravish you right here, right now."

She laughed. She had no such concern for her health, she felt quite well, better than ever, in fact.

"The wedding will be soon," Tom went on. "I will send word, post haste, to Lord Burghley and ask for your hand."

"I am sure my father will answer favourably. He and mother were quite taken with you."

He leaned forward and kissed her brow. "Are you sure you're not still delirious and this is why you've accepted my proposal?"

"It is a possibility." She smiled up at him, her heart filling with love and anticipation of a wonderful life with Tom. "In which case, I will retract it in the morning."

"There will be no retractions." He chuckled. "But we will keep it between us until your father has given his consent."

"That would be the right thing to do." She studied him. His eyes were dancing in the candlelight and full of love and happiness. She was sure he'd see the same reflected back in hers. "Tom." She touched his cheek, tracing the shape she'd carefully painted not long ago. "Will you call for Sarah to help me prepare for the night?"

He appeared slightly surprised by her words. "You are tired? We have exhausted you."

"No." She shook her head. "I just want to be ready...ready for you."

"I don't know what you mean." He stroked her hair, his touch tender.

"I want you to lie with me, tonight. Soon we will be married, we know that." She pulled in a breath, her heart rate picking up. "I don't want to wait, Tom. I want to be with you, the way a woman wants to be with the man she loves."

He was quiet for a moment, then, "Are you sure?"

"As long as you're sure you want me as your wife?"

"I have never been surer of anything, and I would fight to the death anyone who tried to stop it." His tone was firm.

"I know you would." She smiled. "Come to me, later."

"I will." He kissed her gently. "And we will make the night ours, and ours alone."

Elizabeth lay staring at a candle in the corner, the flickering flame dancing in a draught. It was the only light in the room and cast a deep, buttery shadow over the curtains and the chair Tom had sat in during the afternoon.

Sarah had helped Elizabeth bathe and then brushed her hair and carefully applied jasmine cream to her feet and hands. Her nightgown had been fresh on, but the moment Sarah had bid Elizabeth goodnight and left the room, Elizabeth had discarded it, letting it drop to the floor with a quiet whoosh.

The sensation of the sheets on her naked skin was exciting and added to her anticipation. With each tick of the clock on the dresser, she grew more impatient for her husband-to-be to join her.

And then finally the adjoining door opened, and he appeared from around the modesty screen. His white nightshirt hung to his mid thighs and glowed softly in the dim light.

He didn't speak, he went to the main door and flicked the lock. Then he moved to the heavy curtains and opened them just a crack.

At once, the silvery glow of a near full moon spilled in, stretching over the floor and the first inch of the bed.

"I want to be able to see you," he said in almost a whisper.

Elizabeth didn't answer; instead, she watched as he peeled off his nightshirt and draped it over the back of the chair.

A thrill went through her. Her husband-to-be was a fine specimen of a man. Tall, broad-shouldered, defined muscles, and a cock that was hard and ready.

He walked to the bed, the moonlight flashing over his pecs and abs for a split second before he pulled back the covers and slipped beside her.

"My love," he murmured, cuddling her close. "Are you sure?"

"Yes." The warm, erotic sensation of flesh on flesh had her heart skipping a beat, and she wound her arms around him and curled her legs with his.

"I will make it so good for you," he murmured before kissing her.

She melted against him, her breasts pressing onto his chest.

Letting out a small groan, he ran his hand over her left buttock, drawing her closer, trapping his cock between them. It hardened further, a solid wedge she wanted more of.

And then his hands were everywhere, roaming her body; up her back, over her thighs, her behind, her breasts. Her breaths picked up, sensations so sweet she didn't want them to end. But she was impatient for more and explored his body, learning every inch of him.

When she took his erection in her hand and held it firmly, he broke the kiss and groaned again. "Be careful, my need for you is intense."

"So why are you waiting?"

He made a low growling sound and urged her onto her back. But it wasn't his cock that slipped between her thighs, it was his fingers.

Clinging to his shoulders, she stared up at him as he found her entrance and eased one finger in. She was wet for him, ready for him, and she moaned and canted her hips for more.

"My sweet Beth," he said softly against her lips, his stubbled chin scratching hers. "You are ready for a man."

"Yes, my first man, you, the only man I'll ever want."

The stretch in her cunny increased when he added another finger and pushed deep. It was just a taster of what was to come, and she let out a small whimper.

"Am I hurting you?"

"No, no, Tom. I want you. I want you to be inside me, properly." She dug her fingers into the flesh on his shoulders.

"And I will be. Very soon." He kissed her again, working his fingers the way she wanted him to work his cock. Driving in deep then almost withdrawing, the heel of his palm catching on her sweet spot.

Soon she was hot, perspiration peppering her skin. The need for more almost unbearable. "Oh...please..."

He withdrew and hovered over her, hands either side of her head. He studied her face and found her entrance with the tip of his cock.

Cupping his face, she hooked her lower legs around his, holding him close. This was the moment she'd been dreaming of. Tom was the man she'd been dreaming of before she'd even met him. It felt so right to be losing her virginity to him. Soon they'd be wed. Soon this would be their life, every night.

"Relax," he whispered.

She stared at his face, his features gentle in the amber lighting, even though his jaw was set tight.

He prodded forward. For a moment his cock seemed impossibly wide, but then her arousal eased his way, and he filled her the first inch.

"Breathe," he said. "Don't forget to breathe, Beth."

She blew out a breath she didn't even know she'd been holding.

"Are you quite well?" he asked.

"Yes. Yes. I am."

"If I hurt you, you must promise to tell me."

"You're...you're not hurting me." She slipped her hands beneath the covers, ran them down his back and gripped his buttocks. "I want to know what it's like to be a woman, *your* woman."

"You are mine. You will always be mine. I'll never let you go."

"I don't want you to. I...oh..."

He'd curled his hips under, driving his cock deeper into her body. The stretch was almost painful, a nip, a sting, a dense weight. But she took it, wanting them to be as one.

"You feel so good," he said, his voice gravelly. "So hot and tight around me."

Elizabeth didn't answer. She was concentrating on taking him, on not tensing up, as he continued to fill her. How much more could she take?

And then, just when she was about to squirm with the intensity of it, his body grazed up against her, applying pressure to her nub.

"Oh!" She moved on him, stimulating herself further.

"Does it feel good?" he asked.

"So good." She swallowed and urged him down for a kiss.

They kissed, they found a rhythm, a gentle dance of hips and bodies, a slick buildup of pressure. Her sweet spot was swollen and needy, each ride over it taking her towards a moment of sheer bliss. She wanted it to come fast, to wash over her, and she drew her legs higher, wanting him deeper still.

"Aw, strewth, in the name of the Lord." Tom stilled, then withdrew.

"What? What did I do?"

"Nothing, it just feels too good." He closed his eyes tight for a moment and gripped his cock.

"Tom?"

"It's perfectly normal, here, like this." He flopped onto his back, his head sinking deep in the pillow. "Sit astride me."

"Really?"

He smiled and urged her to sit over him. "Aye, I think you'll like it."

The covers slipped, and she sat over him, naked, unsure of what to do.

"Just sit down on my cock," he said. He held it upright. "Take me like this."

"And that will be better for you?"

"It will be good for both of us." His voice was still strained, as though he were harnessing vast amounts of self-control.

"You have done it like this before?" she asked.

"A man needs to know how to please his wife," he said, cupping her right breast and squeezing her nipple. "But I haven't done this with you, the woman I want to spend the rest of my life with. This is special, you're special."

"Oh, Tom." She clasped her hand over his, holding him to her breast, her heart.

"Lower yourself," he said. "Onto me."

She did as he'd asked, taking him deep into her body. The feeling of control was wonderful, empowering, and when she sat fully, she rolled her hips, stimulating her nub. A long groan grated from her chest and throat; she could hardly believe it was her who'd made such a noise.

"Oh aye, like that," he said, his hands covering both her breasts as he stared up at her. "Like that, Beth. Find your pleasure."

"It's so good," she gasped. Her hips seemed to take on a life of their own. She ground over him, rubbing her nub on his hard body. "It's so good."

"Aye." He gritted his teeth. His muscles were like stone, his cock a solid spear inside her.

She sped up, finding the exact place she needed stimulation the most and riding him.

"Darn it, take your pleasure," he gasped.

The dark, desperate tone of his voice sent her over the edge, and she flung back her head, ground onto him, and let the pressure release. She felt wild, wanton and alive, and white-hot bliss shot around her body. Her cunny clamped around his cock over and over, and she had to bite her lip to stop herself from crying out.

Suddenly he lifted her, bowing forward he clutched his cock. A long, guttural groan left his chest as his seed burst from his cock onto his abdomen. He worked his cock, and more seed, thick and glossy, landed on his flesh.

"Tom?" She was hot and breathless. "What...?"

"Aye...that was...darn it." He flopped back, eyes closed, still gripping his cock.

She manoeuvred off of him and lay down at his side, stroked his face. "Did I do something wrong?"

"No, hell no." He turned to her, swallowed, then found her hand and kissed her knuckles. "You were perfect."

"So why...? I don't understand."

"I thought perhaps I should wait until we are wed before spilling my seed inside you."

"Ah...now I see."

"But it was probably one of the hardest things I've ever had to do." He chuckled, though the sound was strained.

"Why?"

"Because you, Lady Elizabeth Burghley, are such a fine, beautiful and responsive woman it is near impossible for me not to want to spill my seed at the first touch of your body against mine."

"I am glad you think me fine."

"The finest." He smiled and kissed her, then gathered her close.

Within his embrace, she closed her eyes and waited for her breathing and heart rate to return to normal.

Tom pulled the covers up to their shoulders, and his breathing slowed and steadied to match hers.

Soon, she was drifting off to sleep in his arms. She'd never felt safer or more content. Her heart was full of love and ripe with hope for the future. A life with Tom was going to be a good life indeed.

She dreamed of Burghley House, her parents, her friends, and soon it merged with Kilead, the mountains, the stags, and the eagles. The two magnificent homes were at harmony together. Sarah's smiling face, a babbling brook the colours of her paints, a carriage rattling around her, a lemon cake, whisky, and then a delicious heat over her back. The heat increased; it was pleasant, and she leaned into it. And then her breasts were being caressed and her nipples tightening.

With a groan, she saw Tom's face in her dream, lit by moonlight, smiling, his hair ruffled and messy. "Tom," she whispered.

"I'm right here." His deep voice came from behind her—she must have turned away from him in her sleep.

A gentle touch between her legs, from behind, and a probing finger.

She groaned softly. She'd been woken by Tom. He was gently touching her breasts, switching between them, and his hot, hard body was curled around hers.

"I want you again, so badly," he murmured. "Once was never going to be enough tonight, not after wanting you for so long."

"I want you, too." She stared at the gap in the curtains. The moon had slipped from view. "I'll want you, always." She parted her legs and reached behind herself to grasp him closer.

"Like this," he said, lifting her top leg. "Let me in from here."

His cock was there, at her cunny, and he didn't wait for her to answer, he just slipped inside her body. There was some resistance, her cunny tight, but after a little adjusting, he drove to full depth.

She whimpered and sank back onto him. The need was intense, all she could think of.

"You feel like Heaven," he whispered. "When I'm with you, I'm in Heaven." He almost pulled out, then eased back in.

She gasped, pushing onto him, then moaned when she didn't get quite what she needed.

"I've got you," he said. He slid his hand over her hip and found her nub. "You'll always get your pleasure when we lie together, never fear."

Before she could answer, he rubbed small circles over her nub, giving her the exact stimulation she needed to combine with his thick cock buried deep.

She closed her eyes and became lost to him. Lost to the way he was driving her closer and closer to release. She gripped his forearm and felt the way the tendons moved as he rotated her nub so expertly.

"Are you close?" he asked hotly into the shell of her ear.

"Yes...oh yes..." Her cunny was slick and quivering. The tip of his cock riding over a deliciously sensitive spot each time he reached full depth. "Don't stop."

"I...won't." He was close, too, his words clipped, his body tense. "Oh... Beth."

"It's...it's there." She pressed down onto his cock, her cunny clamping around his length. Honeyed ecstasy crashed through her.

He groaned, plundered into her, his hips thrusting.

Her climax extended, his desperate need for her his obvious pleasure, tipping her into a new realm of delight.

"My love. My love," he gasped at her ear.

His cock was pulsing, throbbing inside her. She was in the grips of divine spasms that started in her pelvis then wound their way over her skin, tightening her belly and making her breaths hard to catch. "Oh! Oh!" Heat spread inside her, his cock slicker than ever as he ground out his pleasure.

And then he slowed, gradually stopping until his chest rose and fell against her back and his body spooned around hers. He stroked up her belly to cup her right breast.

"Tom," she said and found his hand. She covered it with hers.

"I am sorry," he said onto the nape of her neck.

"Why?"

"I spilled my seed inside you."

She hesitated for a moment, then, "If we have a child a little earlier than planned it will not be of consequence."

"Except to anyone who can count the months." He kissed her neck. "But it will not matter, we will marry before the next full moon if you are agreeable."

"Yes, I am very agreeable to that."

"Then I shall have the banns read and add a note to your parents to plan a trip to Kilead within three weeks if they agree to our union."

"They will agree." She turned within his arms and stroked a lock of hair from his face. She was damp between her legs. "They were already eyeing you up as a future son-in-law. And I saw approval in their faces even if I did not approve of your methods of stealing me away to the wilds of Scotland."

He smiled. "Are you glad you came now? To the wilds?"

"You know full well I am. I am also glad I went into the forest that summer's day in search of flowers."

"And I am glad I asked Gerald to let me use the lodge in the hope of finding inspiration." He paused. "Truth be told, I not only found more inspiration than I thought possible, I also found the other half of my soul."

She smiled and touched her lips to his. That was exactly how it felt. They completed each other, she almost felt as if she'd been lost in the years before she'd met him.

He pulled her close and deepened the kiss. Set his hand over her behind and squeezed.

The sooner the wedding took place the better. Because now they had given in to temptation, there wasn't anything to stop them lying together every night. A babe would soon be made, God willing, and then an heir would be born.

"I love you," he whispered.

"And I love you, from this day until my last."

# About the Author

Based in the UK Lily Harlem is an award-winning, USA Today best-selling author of sexy romance. She's a complete floozy when it comes to genres and pairings writing from heterosexual kink, to gay paranormal and everything in-between. She's also very partial to a happily ever after.

One thing you can be sure of, whatever book you pick up by Ms Harlem, is it will be wildly romantic and deliciously sexy. Enjoy!

Printed in Great Britain
by Amazon

23000967R00106